MW01126568

THE DEVIL'S DUE

OUT OF THE DARK

BOYD CRAVEN

Copyright © 2016 Boyd Craven III

The Devil's Due, Out of the Dark Book 3
By Boyd Craven

Many thanks to friends and family for keeping me writing! Special thanks to Jenn, who has helped me with my covers from day one and keeps me accountable!!!!!

Cover Photo by Phelan A. Davion www.DavionArt.com

To be notified of new releases, please sign up for my mailing list at:
http://eepurl.com/bghQb1

TABLE OF CONTENTS

CHAPTER
1

I'd started throwing up almost as soon as I settled in at the farm. Much of what had happened to me and how I had been rescued was a blur. They'd explained it to me, but my entire body felt like one big sustained cramp which started in my stomach. Even now, I knew it would get worse. The first day was just a warm-up, the next few days would be an utter hell, and I wasn't sure if I could do it.

Breathe. Easy to say, hard to do, especially when you're curled up around the toilet, worried you won't have the strength to lift your head when the nausea becomes too much. I still hadn't seen the doc Steve was talking about. He'd been called away in the middle of our rescue mission to a woman in labor. Part of me raged, the bitter, jealous part of me. I knew she was more important than a useless junkie. If I were in his shoes, I probably would have done the same thing… but I'm me. I'm broken.

"You can't lay there, Dick," a feminine voice told me, trying to lift me from behind my arms.

"Hurts," I said, unable to help myself.

"The doctor just got back. I need you to get on the couch," she said.

I couldn't see her, despite trying to get up. The cramp was all consuming, and it took everything not to plead for something to ease it. Mentally I understood, having gone through it a few times already, but I also knew from the times I'd tried to get clean and had given up, that a quick shot would ease the pain. Even if it was just for a short period.

"I can't," I said. "I just need a minute."

I made it to my knees with her tugging at me, and it was a good thing, because I vomited again, and not on the white tiled floor of the main bathroom. Score one for me.

"You're too big for me to carry. The doc is about a hundred years old, so you've got to do this," she said.

I struggled, and my free hand found a grab bar. It was one of those stainless steel ones made for the elderly. I was lucky that the house had been upgraded before the O'Sullivans had purchased it. That grab bar was the only thing that enabled me to pull myself up. I had been drugged, beaten, and interrogated for more than a week, but that first shot had been enough to get my body rolling down the road of addiction again. It was why I never took pain meds. Not that I could have found them, even if I'd wanted them.

"Ok," I said, gaining my feet.

I could feel her body behind me, how her arms and chest muscles strained to keep me from falling over. Slowly, I straightened up and turned. My entire body was sweating, and I knew it wasn't going to be long before the shakes and the cycle of sweating and then freezing would begin. Then, I got a good look at the woman. It was Courtney.

"What's wrong?" Courtney asked when she saw me looking her over.

"For a second there, I thought you were Jamie," I admitted.

"Dude, you've still got bruises from Steve, don't start this," she whispered, but she was grinning.

"You're going to enjoy this, aren't you?" I asked her seriously.

"Watching you suffer, or picking on you?" She grinned.

"Either," I gasped as she held onto my arm and started walking backwards.

Damn, I hadn't flushed the toilet. I should have taken care of that, but I was moving now, and I didn't know if I could get up again if I fell, so I went with her.

"I don't want to see you suffer," she said seriously, walking slowly. "But the Jamie thing, yeah. I do tease you a little too much. I can stop."

"You know," I gasped, "you're mostly right."

Courtney stopped and looked at me, "You fell in love with her," she said very softly.

BOYD CRAVEN

"I'm in love with Mary," I replied, the house eerily quiet, "but I… You're right, too," I told her seriously, surprised at how loud I was.

The house was an old sprawling farmhouse. White wood siding, modern metal roofing. Half a dozen bedrooms, a basement… a big but claustrophobic kitchen, full of old appliances from a century when power was seldom used. The dining room had been converted into storage, for both the gun lockers and tactical gear. I'd been told that the basement was where the friends and family of Steve and Jamie were housed, with bunk beds stretching across the entire width. Across the stairs from the basement were the stairs leading up to the bedrooms, and a third-floor loft.

Mel had told me all about it, but I had only been on the couch or in the bathroom since I'd arrived. The house had been strangely silent, except for a sudden gasp from the staircase that came down to the main floor. Courtney paled and led me to the couch. Before I started to sit down, I chanced a look over my shoulder and saw a flash of raven hair as somebody retreated back upstairs.

"Was that…?" I asked.

Courtney nodded. "Bad timing. I'm sorry, I didn't know she was inside."

"Not your…" I fell forward onto the couch, almost crushing Courtney with my weight. The cramp had gone from unbearable to absolute evil, and my arms and legs started shaking.

Courtney pushed my body onto the couch, rolled me on my side, and put a bedpan close to my

6

THE DEVIL'S DUE

head. Then she turned around and ran for the front door, calling for the doc. I figured since I was either having a seizure or dying, I'd at least pray for one last chance. Unable to make the words come out, I struggled to even hold them in a thought.

I prayed for the safety of Mary and Maggie, I prayed for my friends, and I prayed that someday, Jamie would forgive me my slip of the tongue. I never should have said it, and I couldn't blame it on the withdrawals or the drugs. At least, to myself I couldn't. The door banged open as I was trying to finish my prayer. Courtney and an elderly man who was wearing a white button up, black slacks, a stethoscope and carrying a doctor's bag, came in. Despite his age, he looked quite spry.

"I'm Soams," the doc said, "Can you hear me?" My legs were twitching, and I was moaning in pain.

I tried to nod, tried to talk. Nothing came out. I blinked both eyes deliberately.

"Good, let me check you over," he said.

I wanted to scream that I was having a seizure. He flashed a penlight into my eyes, took a quick feel of my pulse and nodded, mumbling to himself. For half a heartbeat, the pain felt a little less, and the cramp began to let up just a little bit, so I drew in a deep, shuddery breath.

"Ah hah… doc…" I finally managed.

"Good, not a seizure. You've been through this before?" the doc asked, looking at the needle tracks on my arm.

I blinked big, noticing that at some point, someone had gotten me a large plain white t-shirt. It was

7

wet with sweat and sticking to my skin.

"Then you know, it's going to get worse. Before the power went out, I had rules I had to follow for procedures like this. Now, I'd like to ask you something, and it's going to impact your course of treatment."

"Go," I mumbled out.

"Go? You want me to leave?" he asked.

"No, he meant go on," Courtney told him, and I blinked in agreement.

"Oh, well then. In Canada, their treatment for heroin withdrawals is a little different than here. Here, we use methadone and other drugs to wean you off of it, with intense therapy and psychiatric drugs. It works and works well... the problem is that this treatment benefits the drug companies more than the patients. In one protocol in Canada, the addict is put under sedation and given another drug that purges the heroin's withdrawal effects from the body. The body experiences cold turkey within forty-eight hours and not one to two weeks. Going without sedation is not recommended, ever. Still, you will be sleeping for much of this procedure, and I would be available to monitor your condition. So, do you want the conventional treatment or the quick?"

I trembled. A quick treatment? But it would be worse than this? Sedation was something I'd avoided whenever I was clean because it was always a slippery slope back into addiction. Mentally, I knew I would always be an addict, but this time, I hadn't gone on the smack on my own. It'd been forced on

8

THE DEVIL'S DUE

me. I was hoping that distinction would make a difference. If not to me, then to someone above. I still didn't know if I could live through it. The seizing up was worse this time than it had ever had been at any other time that I'd tried to go clean. It was this that Salina had told me would be the death of me, if I ever got on the drugs again.

I hoped she was wrong, or had been telling me a lie to make me stop.

"I've got everything here," the doc said, pointing to his bag, "and a battery operated IV stand that's in good working order."

I tried to talk, to tell him to give me the second one, but no words came out. Footsteps could be heard, and I looked to the staircase to see both Mel and Jamie coming down. Mel's hair was wet, and she was pulling a brush through it. A gesture so normal and familiar that it hurt to see it. Had Maggie's world changed? Would she have the normal things like food, water, a house to live in? I prayed that they were fine at Mary's parents' house.

"How is he?" Mel asked.

"He's going through withdrawals, the drugs have him talking funny," Courtney said.

As soon as she'd said it, I knew she'd thrown out that lifeline for me. I wasn't going to correct her, but the look on Jamie's face said it all. Something was bothering her, and her usual features had always been joyful.

"Maybe he's just saying what he really means," Jamie offered.

"He hasn't talked to me," the doc said, "He's almost mute from the pain."

"Pain?" Mel said, putting the brush down on the side table and running over to me.

"Cramped," I whispered to her, as she took my hand and gave it a squeeze.

"He was talking and cursing up a blue storm when I got him out of the bathroom and brought him to the couch," Courtney said. "I think he was trying to piss me off deliberately." She dropped me a wink.

From the way she was standing, I was the only one who would see it, and I appreciated it.

"Second," I gasped out as another cramp seized my body.

The doc held the bedpan as nausea took control of me, and then went to the bathroom to dispose of it.

"Want me to get Luis?" Courtney asked.

I took a deep breath to answer and then realized that very fact was calming. The cramp was losing its hold again. I took a couple of breaths more as the doctor came out. I felt bad, but I was able to talk for a moment.

"Doc, I want the second protocol," I said wheezing, "I'm going to sleep it off?"

"Good, yes. You will sleep during it. I don't have the typical anesthesia I would at a hospital, but I have stuff here that'll do the trick. My only concern is that somebody needs to sit with you the entire time. I can't do that, not with sixty people here on the property."

I thought it must be the drugs that had me hear-

10

ing that wrong. *Sixty? I hadn't seen that many people, and the basement couldn't have held that many.*

"I'll do it," Jamie said, not meeting my eyes.

"I can help," Mel said.

"I'll do it," Courtney said to Jamie. "You've been away from your husband for a while. Besides, another knock on the noggin from your husband will make Dick look like he's got horns."

I hadn't seen myself in the mirror yet, but I figured that was why the doc had checked my eyes. Most of the time when you get knocked out, there's some sort of concussion. Probably trying to gauge how much of this was withdrawal and how much of it was from the abuse and a knockout punch.

"Really, it's no problem—"

"I got this," Courtney said, kneeling down by me and taking my other hand.

Mel gave me a pat on the shoulder and let my hand go, wrapping her arms around her mother.

"But—"

"I still haven't paid Dick back for rescuing me," Courtney explained, "I'd really like to do this. I need to do this."

"Oh," Jamie said in a small voice, "I understand. I just… it's hard to see somebody hurting like this."

"That's another reason for letting me do it. It's going to be bad," Courtney told her.

Jamie looked to the doc, who nodded in confirmation.

"Well, let's get some of the men in here to carry you up to the guest room," the doc said. "You'll be taking the bigger guest room with the adjoining bathroom for the next few days. You and the young lady… Courtney is it?" She nodded in agreement. "Courtney will need to be comfortable. She probably won't get much sleep, but I've already cleared it with Mr. O'Sullivan."

I nodded mutely, and Courtney got to her feet. I understood part of what she was doing, even in my addled state. She was paying off a debt, and keeping me away from Jamie for the time being. Until I was more stable, I couldn't be around her. Mistaking her for Mary in front of her husband was one thing, but I knew that the quick exchange with Courtney had more truth to it than I was comfortable with. Until that moment, I hadn't even fully admitted it to myself. At least Jamie hadn't heard me say the words.

I sighed in relief as the cramp passed.

"So, guys," I said in a surprisingly calm voice, "What happened to you, and how did you all escape and…?"

"Rest," Courtney told me, "We'll fill you in until the doc comes back."

CHAPTER 2

That kid who turned us in, he rode in the Hummer with us," Mel told me. "He'd been found and taken into the FEMA camp, and when he described you to the security there, they got really interested."

"Why?"

It was Jamie who answered. "There's somebody down south who's been raising hell with FEMA camps, freeing prisoners. I guess we were about two hours from one of the larger camps, and they had already been on heightened alert. That's why the Hummers were out there."

"They questioned us all, one by one, and they took you away to a separate place," Courtney said. "We told them your name and what little we knew. I didn't think it would hurt. I'm sorry they tortured you. I didn't know that telling them would be so bad," she said, turning as the door opened and Luis strode in.

Seeing her crying, he walked over and used his thumb to wipe away a tear that was rolling down her cheek.

"I wasn't the guy who they were looking for," I said. "Somehow, they had me mixed up with somebody I used to know."

"What?" Luis asked.

"Yeah, John Norton. He's a retired SEAL. Got a son who's a missionary somewhere in South America, I think."

"So the whole thing, what they did to you, was pointless?" Mel asked.

"I don't remember a lot of it," I lied. "Things are blurry, but I remember that. They kept saying I was already dead. Being in a cell with them, I knew I was a dead man who still had a heartbeat. But you got me out," I said looking at Jamie. "Thanks."

She nodded at me. "Well, during the processing, I saw somebody walk past in a sheriff's uniform, and I called out to him. It was a deputy who recognized Mel and me. He made a call on his radio and after Steve came out, then they became a lot nicer with us."

"Wait, your husband was working for them?" I asked, confused.

She nodded. "The entire department that my husband ran were ordered to work there, by executive order," she said, rolling her eyes. "But they were ready to leave with their families. It wasn't horrible

THE DEVIL'S DUE

in there, for what little time I was there, but nobody was free to go, except for the bus drivers and the guards, who brought in more people. The deputies worked as an internal police force for DHS and FEMA. I guess some camps have NATO advisors. Like that guy that we heard on the radio."

I nodded weakly. "So, what happened when you recognized the deputy?"

"My dad came up," Mel answered, "yelling and screaming at the soldiers. I guess one of the perks of working there, is that the families don't have to do the same work as everyone else, and no rough handling…"

"Was he surprised?" I asked, despite myself.

"Yeah, after he knocked out the guy who was trying to get his superior on the radio… he wasn't moving fast enough for Steve. After that, it was a few days of finding out where you were, and then we broke out."

"We?" I asked.

"All of the sheriff's department, their families, and anybody else we could take with us. It was kind of horrible. There was a NATO group nearby, one with a ton of Hummers and a big armored truck thingy with a cannon on top. Anyway, they chased us for a while, but we got here, got things set up, and then came for you when we could."

"I only saw a dozen or so people when you guys broke me out…" I winced, the cramps coming back. My toes curled so hard, they popped like I was breaking bones.

Courtney sat down with me, pulling my arms

15

to my side. I wasn't actually controlling them, but they were tight against my chest.

"Breathe through it," she told me.

Everyone waited, and within a moment, it passed again. I was drenched in sweat and starting to shiver.

"There were about thirty people in on the assault of the base you were at," Luis said. "We had to stay behind, but just about every other deputy or male on the premises here went out. It was almost too easy. It was like they wanted you to have an easy way to get out."

"Trust me, I probably wasn't going anywhere. Even if I'd gotten outside... I think they were only there to keep me in, not repel a significant force."

"They had a surprise," Mel said, "My dad talked about that. He did the thing you had the town do when the ambush was set up for those raiders, except he didn't use bait, just somebody blowing a police whistle."

"What would have happened if they had used the Hummers?" I asked them.

"I guess they would have used the ones that we took in our getaway. One of them is armored, but none of them have big guns like the ones that caught us on the side of the road," Courtney said.

I was tired and getting more so. Still, from experience, I knew that I wouldn't sleep. I never could when I'd gone through withdrawals. Instead, I'd gone to the hazy gray world where I wanted to sleep, but could never quite get there.

"But they got me out," I gasped as another

16

THE DEVIL'S DUE

cramp started.

"Yeah, and here we are—home," Jamie said, giving me a brief smile and meeting my gaze for the first time.

I tried to smile back. Maybe she believed the story about being a drug-withdrawal-induced jabber jaw.

"In here," I heard and then the door opened, and Doc Soams walked in with three men, one of which was Steve.

"Wait, earlier you said the deputies worked for your Steve?" I asked Jamie.

"Well yeah, he's the County Sheriff," she answered.

Huh. When they'd told me what he did, I'd thought they meant he was *a* sheriff, as in a deputy. I hadn't caught on that he was *THE* Sheriff.

"Telling stories about me?" Steve asked, coming over to the couch and standing at the foot.

My friends backed up to give him room. I looked at the stairwell and then back at them. He did the same thing.

"Stairwell is too narrow to do more than one person at a time," he told me. "Can you walk?"

"A little," I gasped as a wave of nausea had me suddenly dry heaving.

"Well, don't get any on me," Steve said as he pulled my arm over his shoulder and lifted at the waist in a fireman's carry.

I half expected to get hit as we went through the doorway to the stairs, but I was wrong. Instead, I felt the up and down swaying motion that made me

17

think of boat rides.

"Let me get him situated and then everyone can come in," Steve said over his shoulder.

It was at least a dozen steps from the stairs to a small bedroom. I could see it, albeit upside down. A little cloth chair sat next to a twin sized bed. A candle and a box of matches had been placed on the nightstand beside it. Another open doorway revealed the connecting bathroom. Then, I was placed right side up and on the bed. I looked up and saw the Sheriff was sweating from the effort. He got some deep breaths in before he leaned down.

"Listen, I want to thank you for getting Jamie and Mel back to me. I was slowly going crazy without knowing. After so long, I'd thought they were probably dead. I mean, I'd been getting reports about Michigan, and that it was pretty much a dead state in most spots. So I really appreciate it." He put his hand out, and it took all of my strength to take it and shake it.

Before letting go, he leaned in close to me. "But as soon as you're healthy… I want you to move on, and *stay away from my wife*."

Maybe I hadn't fooled anybody. Shit.

"Yeah, as soon as I can, Courtney, Luis, and I are headed to Arkansas."

"I'm not asking them to move on," he said, and let go of my hand, and backed up and walked out of the door. Message received.

The doc was the first one in, struggling with something tall and chrome. It took me a second to realize it was an IV stand, with several bags already

18

set up. Then, folks started coming in.

"I'm going to sit with him for this," Courtney told Luis.

"I figured you would," he replied.

She raised an eyebrow and leaned in. He kissed her, and I jumped with a sudden jolt of pain as the doc stuck a needle in my arm, the site wet from the alcohol swab. I hadn't even felt him working until the needle had gone in.

"Sorry, I normally have phlebotomists or nurses to do the IVs. I'm a little out of practice." He taped a bandage over the IV.

He hit a few buttons, and I felt the cold sensation of the solution entering my body. Strangely, it seemed like the opposite of when I would shoot up; the smack always felt hot. Too hot. Maybe it was because of the different protocol. I couldn't remember, and I didn't know what was in it, I just trusted the doc to make me well again. If I didn't die that was; Salina's words still hung over my head.

"So, now what do we do?" Courtney asked.

"Well, as soon as I put this into his IV," Doc Soams pulled out a preloaded syringe, "he'll fall asleep. Then I'll turn the drip on. After that, it's just time and keeping him from pulling the IV out."

"I thought you were going to sedate him?" Mel asked.

"He'll probably have some shaking fits. Those are normal, but it's the convulsions that I'm worried about. If it goes on for too long, I have Ativan to administer, or I can leave it here for whoever's going to sit with him."

19

BOYD CRAVEN

"If you tell me the dose, I can do it," Courtney offered.

"Sure, it's not brain surgery," the doc said, laughing at his own joke.

His laughter shut off abruptly when he realized nobody else was laughing, and that alone made me smile.

"Ok, so... I'll be here for the first hour after sedation, to make sure there's no reaction. Then I have a baby that I need to go check on," he said, putting the needle of sedative into the inlet of the IV, and pushing the plunger down.

"How long will it be to take effect?" I asked him, feeling resigned to whatever fate I had. Live or die.

"You should be feeling it soon. You'll just fall asleep. Everybody should say your goodbyes now; he'll be out for a couple days at least."

"See you soon, I hope," I told them, and almost as a chorus, everyone said goodbye. Courtney flopped down on the chair next to the bed as she said hers.

"Count down from ten," Doc said.

"Ten."

I didn't want to die, but I knew the odds were against me.

"Nine."

I wanted to hold Mary once again, and plead with my daughter not to hate me for being such a lousy father.

"Eight."

I prayed that I wouldn't end up a vegetable, and make the O'Sullivan's responsible for me.

20

THE DEVIL'S DUE

"Seven," I said, my eyelids heavy.

The cramp was there, but it wasn't knocking the breath out of me as bad.

"Six."

The brief kiss I'd shared with Jamie.

"Fiv—"

I felt my head slumping.

"He's out," Doc said, and even though I wasn't all the way there yet, I heard him.

* * *

I was throwing up so violently, my stomach felt like it was being turned inside out. I was crying, and a woman was holding onto me, holding me upright in her lap, pleading with me to hold still. Pain. Doc was putting in another syringe into the IV. I saw this through slit eyes. Salina's words repeated in my head over and over.

* * *

I had the shakes, but could feel the warmth of somebody sitting close to me. A hand was running through my hair. A cool cloth brushed over my brow. I didn't want to die.

* * *

Doc was putting another shot into the IV. Whatever it was, it was going to kill me…

CHAPTER
3

I smelled smoke. My body hurt as if I'd been working out and had really overdone it. My stomach felt like it had been scraped clean, turned inside out, and then scrubbed with rusty barbed wire. Still, I felt the pangs of hunger, not the overwhelming nausea that had been plaguing me. I looked at my arm and saw the IV still in it. I looked up and saw an empty bag of saline. Two more things came to me in a flash. I wasn't alone in the bed, and I had to piss so bad I was worried I wouldn't make it to the bathroom.

Pushing myself up, I grabbed the IV stand. I didn't know how long I'd been out for, and my thoughts were muddied from the sedation. I sort of remembered waking up, unless that had been a dream. I didn't know. Still, I saw nothing plugged

THE DEVIL'S DUE

into the IV stand so being careful, I rolled it to the open bathroom door with me in tow. My legs still felt shaky, and I was weak, but somehow I'd come out the other end. I hit the lever to flush the toilet and was surprised when it went down. I'd done it on auto pilot and then, had been surprised when it worked. I tried the lights with no success.

Getting back to the bed was a little more work than I'd imagined. Especially, considering the way the woman was sprawled out across it, now that I wasn't in it. I pulled one end of the covers up and saw it was Courtney. She was sleeping the sleep of the utterly exhausted, or the half dead. I let the covers drop, and she pulled them over her shoulder and rolled into the middle, making a mumbling sound. I hadn't died. That's when I saw the half-eaten sandwich and a glass of water. Probably hers.

She wouldn't mind, so I ate it and marveled… I hadn't died. I sat down in the chair with that thought in my mind. Somehow, I was on the other side. God, I wanted some smack, but no worse than at any other moment. I could usually deal with the mental stuff, it was just when the physical side of it hurt so badly, making me sick, that I would lose my nerve and shoot up again. It wasn't an option, and I didn't want to go through with that hell again. Even if it had been a breeze this time.

Looking around, I saw that the window over-looking the yard had a spider crack, with a strip of duct tape over it. It hadn't been that way before. Also, there was a big chunk out of the plaster across from the window, to the right of where I was sitting.

I turned my neck to look at it, and the realization hit me. Somebody had shot into the room while I was out of it.

"You're up on your own? They told me you were a fighter," Doc Soams said, walking into the bedroom with a steaming mug of what smelled like coffee.

"I feel like hammered shit," I admitted, reaching out for the cup.

The doc hesitated. "Here," he said, "I was going to have a cup, but I wasn't expecting you up already."

I started to hand it back, and he put his hands up as if to tell me to stop. "No, it's ok. Normally, I wouldn't have somebody who went through what you just did start on coffee. Actually, the soup would be better, but I think you might need it," he said, looking at the now empty plate.

"Thanks," I said, my voice strangely hoarse.

Have you ever had the world's best ice cream cone on a day that's so hot, and your throat is so parched? That's what it felt like as soon as I took the first sip of the coffee. I closed my eyes and took another. I felt something on my chest and opened my eyes to see the doc holding the end of his stethoscope over my heart.

"If you feel up to it, I'll pull the IV out."

"I feel hungover," I told him. "But about a thousand percent better than when I was laid down." I took another sip… it was heavenly. "How long was I out?"

"Three days, instead of two. You had a reaction,

THE DEVIL'S DUE

so I had to give you antihistamines and epineph-rine," the Doc said, his gaze going to the left as he talked to me.

Liar. What was he lying about?

"I'm doing ok now?" I asked.

"Yes. Your friend is pretty worn out, though. Don't be surprised if she sleeps half the day, now that you aren't thrashing about."

"Was it bad?" I asked.

"It's never easy." He pulled the bandage back from my IV.

He got the supplies out, removed the IV, cov-ered the site with a cotton ball, and then a Band-Aid. When I'd been shooting up myself, I'd rarely even covered it with a Band-Aid. A thumb was used until it quit bleeding. No wonder I had scars from getting infected.

"I smell smoke," I told him. A statement, not a question.

"We've had some problems. It kept me from giv-ing you some of the doses of the sedative on time."

The reason I kept waking up, I thought.

"What kind of problems?"

"Soldiers, or DHS. I don't know which."

"So, how bad was it?"

"Eleven."

"Eleven, what?" I asked.

"Eleven dead."

His words chilled me.

"Who? Jamie, Mel—"

"Mostly our people," the doc said somberly.

"Mostly?" I thundered, trying not to panic, not

screaming for fear of waking Courtney.

"Her man, Luis…" he said, looking at Courtney, "…he went to the fence line to pull Sheriff O'Sullivan out of the line of fire. He'd been hit, and Luis dragged him to a fortified spot. One of the goons opened up with a SAW. There was nothing I could do."

The sudden sense of loss hit me hard. I wasn't best friends with him, but we'd been together for the trip here, and I'd known him from the market, and then more when he'd become Courtney's man. I couldn't figure out if I wanted to scream or to cry. Probably both.

"Is Steve dead?" I asked.

The doc shook his head no. "He had a grazing wound in his thigh. The other one was mostly a through and through. He's stable, but sleeping."

"Who else? Jamie and Mel?" I repeated.

"They're fine. Working themselves to the bone, helping me take care of the injured."

I sighed in relief, yet a tear for Luis slid down my cheek. I would have to be careful, or I'd turn on the waterworks. Grief was a feeling I knew all too well. Grief and feeling helpless.

"How's she doing?" I asked, pointing to Courtney.

"If she didn't have you to take care of, I'd probably have her on a suicide watch." The doctor's words were delivered in the quietest voice yet. "She took it really hard. She said they'd been talking about Texas, and starting a family when the world settled down some."

THE DEVIL'S DUE

"Where are they? The O'Sullivans?" I asked.

"They're all in the master suite currently. It's at the end of the hallway. I just checked on Mr. O'Sullivan's leg."

"Ok, thanks, doc," I said, pulling myself to my feet.

"You may want to get cleaned up first," he said. "There's a change of clothes on the sink."

"There's running water here?" I asked.

"Yes, and propane for the water heater. But if you are going to shower, keep it short. You know what Navy showers are?"

I nodded. "Doc, I'm sorry I've brought this on everyone. I just hope you all can forgive me."

"You think everything's your fault," a voice said from under the covers.

"Hey, you're awake?" I asked, pulling the cover back to reveal Courtney's red eyes and tear-stained cheeks.

"I was dreaming of him," she said, "and then I woke up and realized that he wasn't here."

She was one of the toughest ladies I'd ever known, but she looked broken. Probably the same look I wore all the time. There was a hint of grief in her eyes, but despite the tears, she looked flat, emotionless. Empty. Broken.

"I'm so sorry," I told her.

She nodded and swung her legs out of bed, throwing the covers aside.

"Life happens," she said in a quiet voice, "the living keep on living. Until they don't."

I didn't have much to say to that, so I nodded.

"Thanks, Doc," I said, standing close to Courtney.

"I'll be back in a couple hours to check on you, but I have other patients. Others injured in the fight. I'll see you soon."

I waved a little dismissively and watched as he turned and left the room. The old man had lost the spring in his step that I'd seen three days ago.

"Do you want to talk about it?" I asked her quietly.

She shook her head.

"Ok. I'm going to take a quick wash up."

"I'll help," she started to follow me.

"I think I got it," I told her, walking slowly so I wouldn't get dizzy and fall.

"I'll wait at the door then, till you get in."

"Do you need to talk?" I asked again, realizing that she was trying to stay close to me, not necessarily to help me wash up.

She nodded. "It's all gone wrong somehow," she said. "I don't want to be alone."

I turned around and stumbled back to her, pulling her close to me and hugging her as hard as I dared. Her sobs came and were mostly drowned out in my shoulder. Still, I held her close. After a few moments, she backed up.

"You smell," she told me.

"That's why I'm going to the shower," I said grinning, "and you're kind of ripe yourself."

"That's because I fell asleep next to you, holding the puke bucket. Don't use the hot water up." She almost laughed, but instead, it turned into a hic-

THE DEVIL'S DUE

cupping sob.

"Promise," I told her, noticing that she was crying again.

* * *

Clean up went fast. As soon as I was in the shower, Courtney walked in and sat on the toilet, staring at the floor. We didn't talk. I washed up in a rush, loving the feel of being clean again and using real soap. After I had turned the water off from my rinse, she left. Once I dressed, she came back in and started stripping down. I left in a hurry, and when the water started, I cracked the door open and asked her if she wanted me to stay out or come back in. The doctor's words rang in my head. Suicide watch. Her not wanting to be alone.

"Please," was all I got from her.

I took her spot, sitting on the toilet until the water turned off and then exited, closing the door. She joined me moments later, wearing sweat pants and a white cotton shirt, the same as had been left out for me. She hadn't taken the time to dry her hair, and it was making her shirt wet across her back. She started tossing the towel down, but I snagged it and gave her hair a brief rubdown, the way I would with Maggie's.

"You want the comb?" she asked.

I stared at her, and then smiled when I got what she'd meant. I used to brush Mouse's hair when I got worked up or upset. It was the little girl's superpower: distract the tall people, keep them talking, make them feel better. Courtney had been there for a lot of Mouse's superpowers while I'd healed, after breaking her and another group of ladies out and hustling them away from a sadistic gang.

"No thanks, I'm good," I told her.

"I'm not, not really, but I'll survive. Don't let the doctor scare you. I heard what he said."

"If you want me to comb your hair…"

She shook her head and opened the door to the hallway. My attempt at a joke had failed. Hard. She waited for me to get out of the doorway before leading the way. Every step closer to the O'Sullivans room filled me with dread. Did this attack on his home and compound happen because they'd broken me out and shot up the DHS goons? Were they coming after them for getting out of the FEMA camp with people and vehicles? Why were they holding and processing people? I had so many questions still.

"Here," she said, pointing at the door at the opposite end of the hall.

The upper floor, I noticed for the first time, had a beautiful wide hall that ran center through it, with the staircase intersecting, making a T shape. Several doors were on each side, with a larger ornate oak door at the end where Courtney had led me. I knocked and heard a soft, "Come in."

"Hey Dick, hi Courtney," Mel said standing up and walking toward me.

"Mel," I murmured.

The bedroom was set up the same way as the guest room I was in was, but a bit larger. A queen

THE DEVIL'S DUE

size bed dominated the center of the room with two chairs facing each other, near a window that overlooked what looked like a lush field of hay or tall grass. Steve was sleeping on top of the bed, a thin blanket pulled over him. Lying next to him was Jamie, one arm wrapped protectively around him. Her eyes were looking at me over his snoring form.

"How is your dad?" I asked her.

"He's going to be ok. We got lucky that the Doc was a prepper, too. He had all kinds of medicine stocked up."

Jamie disentangled herself slowly, so as not to awaken her husband and walked over, wrapping Courtney in a hug and burying her face in Courtney's hair.

"How are you holding up?" I heard her whisper.

Courtney's shoulders hitched again as she started to sob softly.

"How are *you* feeling?" Mel asked me, looking first at her mom and Courtney and then back at me.

"Horrible," I admitted, "but I'll live."

I regretted the words as soon as I'd spoke them. I knew how insensitive it must've sounded. Hollow and empty.

"Hey, we're glad you're ok," Jamie said, breaking her embrace with Courtney and giving me a quick hug.

"Dick, I'm glad to see you on your feet. God, we need your help," Jamie said.

That was like a bucket of cold water thrown on my head.

31

BOYD CRAVEN

"You've got it," I said. "Other than the DHS goons, what else?"

"That's just it. The deputies here are good, but they're not soldiers. We were lucky in stopping the first two pushes. I'm worried they'll be back again."

"Wait, the farm was attacked twice?" I asked.

"Yeah," Mel said, "it's been sort of rough."

"Hey, you're alive," Steve said, making us all turn to look.

He was pulling himself into a sitting position, one leg heavily bandaged.

"Mostly," I said. "How are you holding up? Doc told me you caught two rounds."

"First one grazed me, second went through the meaty part," he said.

His body was covered in sweat, much the same way mine had been when I'd felt the withdrawal coming on.

"They always go through a meaty part," I said deadpan, and he gave me a weak smile.

"My wife is right. We need your help." He stated it as a fact, rather than a question.

What about moving on when I'm healed up? I thought to myself. I mean, he'd made it clear, but had that been the irrational, emotional part of him talking before, or was it his rational part, knowing the trouble that I'd bring to the group?

"I'll help," I told him, "but your rescuing me has brought this on. Are you sure you don't want me to leave?"

Jamie looked to me and then to her husband, and went over and sat down next to him. Steve mo-

32

tioned for me to take a seat. Courtney sat on the foot of the bed, Mel took the other chair. We both turned to look at the bed.

"No," he said, rubbing a hand across his face. "They would have come for me, no matter what. I was barely tolerated by the DHS, but they had orders and so did I… Until we broke out. I had hoped that with our numbers that they wouldn't have even tried this."

"We're vulnerable here," I told him. "All it'd take is some mortars positioned and a forward observer to walk the rounds in. I was out for most of the trip in here, but from what I can see from the windows, the land is pretty flat for miles."

He nodded. "I've got my men watching a five-mile grid around here. We're the only place left in the area with folks, so any movement or people would get called in. It'd buy us enough time to make it to the bunker."

"So what happens if they take out your sentry from long range, and then walk in and set up? Do you have enough coverage to stop that from happening?"

I wasn't trying to be a dickhead, but I suspected that was how I was coming across, judging by the looks on Jamie's and Steve's faces. Mel just looked at me blankly.

"I don't know," he said after a long pause. "That's why I need help. I know police action, but I don't know what the military is going to do."

"Those DHS weren't military. As little as I saw when you guys busted me out, I could see that they couldn't have held up to a crack military unit."

"Yeah, but it's not just DHS who came in. Some of their fallen were wearing NATO gear and patches…"

Then it came to me, the foreign voice on the radio… and, of course, there had always been rumors since the Patriot Act had been voted in, that NATO would be used as a police action in the USA because the government couldn't trust our own military. *Their* oath was to the people and the Constitution. Those who believed that were generally thought to be paranoid, tinfoil hat wearing types. But now, I was seeing that many of them could have pegged everything correctly.

"I don't think I'm in fighting shape today," I admitted, "but once I get some food in me, I think I could walk around and start looking at things. How the property is set up. Maybe come up with a plan before we do some recon?"

"Recon?" Jamie and Steve chorused.

"Dick is probably going to hit them first, if possible," Mel said. "It's what he did in Chicago."

"He did what?" Steve asked.

"I'll let your ladies fill you in," I said, feeling dizzy. "You should rest. I'll come back up here when I know more."

"Ok, good. Talk to Daniel Wright. He's my righthand man. I think he's either at the bunker in the barn or at the front gate. Having me down is probably making him run around like crazy…"

"Just so we're clear," I asked, "I'm going to help, but if we're attacked right now, how many people

34

THE DEVIL'S DUE

here can be expected to fight?"

"All of us," Steve said. "Even me. I think… I'm worried that the time for negotiations between us and them is over. It isn't just that they want you. It's the fact that we broke out right under their noses, and left them vulnerable inside. The camp wasn't that well-protected to begin with."

"How bad was it in there?" I asked.

Mel answered, "It wasn't bad for us, but we weren't there long. People had to work, though: firewood, gardening, cleaning…"

"That doesn't sound so bad," I said. "Everyone working for their dinner and housing?"

"Sort of," Jamie cut in. "But you couldn't just leave if you wanted to, and if you didn't get your quota of work done, you didn't eat. There were rules there that were tricky, so if you messed up, you'd have to go to the detention side of the camp."

"Detention? The whole camp sounds like a prison."

"As true as that is," Steve said, his eyes half closing, "detention was worse. With Martial Law, they could do anything. A firing squad used to be normal. Now, they are saving ammunition because hanging people is cheaper. They can reuse the rope."

"You let this go on?" I asked, surprised.

Jamie and Mel both turned to look at Steve, whose eyes opened wide. He didn't look happy at my question.

"What was I supposed to do?" he demanded angrily, almost growling the words out.

"I don't know, Steve. What did your oath to

35

your badge ask you to do?" I asked standing up, and started walking toward the door on wobbly feet.

"I'll come with you," Courtney murmured, moving to follow.

"My oath?!" Steve spat. "A fat lot of good it did when there were no more laws to enforce, except what the government told us. When I got a chance to get people out, I did. What would you have done differently?"

I knew his question was supposed to be rhetorical, but I answered him anyway.

"I would have killed the traitors, to a man. I would have burned them alive, blown them up, or shot them."

"So, you're a one-man fucking Army?" Steve asked, sarcasm dripping from every word.

"No, sir," I said, making it sound like it was spelled like 'cur'. "I'm a rifleman first, a Marine second, and a Devil Dog to the end." I started walking again.

I could sense movement behind me, and guessed it was Mel moving closer to the bed to talk to her dad. I could hear parts of a hushed conversation as Courtney pulled the door closed.

"I don't think he realizes that you were serious," she drawled.

I turned and looked at her. For once her eyes were dry, but her cheeks still had lines of moisture drying on them.

"Most people never take me seriously," I told her. "Especially, when I'm everything they don't want to see kissing their wife. Junky, bastard, a re-

36

minder of their own failures."

"What was that you asked him about wanting you to stay?"

"Right before treatment, he told me to move on as soon as I healed up. He didn't want me around Jamie."

"I don't know whether that's funny or not," she said.

"Not ha-ha funny, but I don't blame him."

"You're going to blame yourself for all of this, aren't you?"

"Pretty much," I said. "That's why I'll stay and help, even though it burns his ass. Part of it is my fault."

"How do you figure that?"

"I wasn't watching the road behind us, as I should have been. Then, there was the whole bringing NATO into it when they broke me out, killing everyone in the interrogation compound."

"You really think they would have allowed us to just escape with everyone else? We had to get you, and it was my fault for giving them your name. If I hadn't, maybe they wouldn't have been so hard on you, and then when we broke you out, they attacked. I lost Luis," Courtney was almost whispering now. "It's kind of our fault," she said as I stepped off the bottom stair.

The downstairs was bustling with people and activity, unlike three days ago when I had been brought in. The couch had been pushed back against the wall, and three men were laying on sleeping pads, blood-stained bandages covering various body parts. I could hear some banging in the kitchen, and the smell of something heavenly was drifting out. I headed that way, and Courtney put a steadying arm on my shoulder when I wobbled. The sandwich half hadn't been enough, and I was weak with nausea and hunger.

"Easy," she said, "I can't pick you up."

"I'm a little light-headed. I need more food. Oh, I uh… ate your part of a sandwich that was left."

"That's ok," she said. "I wasn't hungry."

I understood that. Grief and loss often manifested in a lot of ways, loss of appetite being one of them. In the short term, it didn't hurt anything, but I worried she'd let this become something all-consuming. I knew the difference between revenge and justice, but sometimes a little bit of both worked well in a situation like this. In the meantime, we had work to do, once we got squared away with some grub.

"Well, you should eat," a portly woman said, coming out of the kitchen wearing a red and white checkered apron.

Her cheeks were ruddy, and she used a wooden spoon to point and punctuate her words. Curly red and gray hair peeked out of the edges of a baseball cap that'd been put there to hold the hair out of her face. It was a Cornhuskers hat. I smiled.

"She probably should," I said.

"Who are you?" she asked, turning the spoon on me.

"Dick Pershing, ma'am, and I was coming down to see about some grub."

38

THE DEVIL'S DUE

She gave me a once over and then asked, "You the junky who was detoxing upstairs?"

I heard Courtney gasp, but I was nodding. I wasn't ashamed. I'd given up my dignity when I'd let my wife walk out of my life because I couldn't control myself.

"Yes, ma'am. All good now."

"Your hands are shaking."

"He hasn't eaten for three days," Courtney reminded her.

"Well, I'll get him a bowl, but you have to eat, too. You haven't eaten a full meal since… well, come on, you two."

I noticed the woman hadn't finished the thought, and I appreciated it. By the smell of things, something with tomato and basil was being cooked. Walking in behind her, I squeezed past a young boy who was spooning noodles into a bowl while the ruddy-faced woman tipped a ladle full of spaghetti sauce on top, making two quick bowls.

"Sebastian, this is Dick and Courtney. They're guests of the O'Sullivans."

I looked at the kid and realized the connection immediately. A son or close nephew. Freckles dotted his face, and his red hair was cropped close to his skull.

"Pleasedtomeetcha," he said all in one word, handing us bowls.

"Hey," Courtney said.

I just smiled. He was about Pauly's age. I gave him a nod and solemnly, he gave me a nod in return.

39

"Now, head out to the porch to eat. I'll have the next shift in here in moments, and I don't have room for you to lollygag about." She made a shooing movement, flicking sauce with every hand gesture.

We fled the kitchen, and as we got to the door, I asked, "Who was that?"

"Beth, one of the neighbors. I guess she takes care of most of the baking and cooking. Just took over. I think Steve is scared of her."

I looked at a random fleck of red staining my shirt and used my thumb to wipe it up, then I licked it off. Sauce.

"I can see how that happened," I said. "If this is half as good as it smells…"

We sat down on a long bench made out of 2x8s that ran along the front porch of the house on either side of the doors. We weren't the only ones eating out there; there were several other men, women, and children. Many of the men and one of the ladies wore the sheriff's department uniform. A few months into the collapse of the world, and there were still cops in clean uniforms. It amazed me. I dug in and found that the food tasted fantastic.

I tried not to lick the bowl clean when I was done, but my stomach was growling. I didn't think I'd ever had anything that good in my life. I looked up to see Courtney smiling for the first time. Outright smiling, as I cleaned up the bowl.

"I told you, she took over."

"I thought it was because of her personality," I said, wiping my mouth with a free hand.

THE DEVIL'S DUE

"That was the original reason, I was told," she said, her face going blank again.

"You finish that up," I said pointing to the bowl.

"I'm not hungry."

"If you want to kill the guys who attacked and hurt so many, you're going to need your strength."

Her eyes grew wide, and she held the bowl up to her mouth, almost gagging as she shoveled the pasta and sauce in. She didn't lick the bowl, but after a couple attempts to hold the food down, she calmed and stood, silent tears streaming down her cheeks.

"You want some payback?" I asked her.

She nodded, wiping at her eyes.

"Let's go turn these in and check out the defenses of this place."

CHAPTER

4

I didn't find Daniel Wright in the bunker under the barn, nor at the gate. The deputies at the gate told us that he was walking the perimeter. A forty-acre fenced-in perimeter. I wasn't sure I was strong enough yet to walk it all, but I was going to try.

"I need to stop a second," Courtney said, pulling a canteen out and taking a drink before handing it to me.

I took a drink myself, washing down the last of the taste of the pasta, and gave it back. I checked on the action of the AR-15, one of the farm's standard guns. I'd taken it right from the front room where the safes were. I was told they were for the defense of the farm, so I made sure to get one and a couple of mags. I found out that if I didn't tie my sweatpants tightly, the mags pulled the sweats off my ass, so I carried a spare one in my left hand.

"Dick, I was wondering…"

"Yeah?"

"How long… I mean… you and Mary. I know she's not dead like Luis, but how long did it hurt? When you two split."

There were no secrets between us, and the once fierce woman was now a shadow of what she'd sounded like when I'd first met her.

"It still hurts, but every day I accept it a little more. I don't want to, I want her to be right here right now… but it doesn't feel like somebody sitting on my chest as much, as time passes."

She leaned forward, letting her head rest on my shoulder for a moment. I was about to pull her close for comfort, but she already was moving back.

"I love him still," she said.

"I know. That's why we're going to kill the fuckers who attacked us, and bust open the FEMA camp."

"You were out of it, but we were barely able to hold them off," Courtney said. "I had to leave your side to fight."

We started walking the fence line, and I could see a figure in the distance.

"How did they come at this place?" I asked her.

"Up to the main gate. Asked questions first, then made demands. Steve made a show of force, and they backed off, only to hit us later on with no warning."

"Big guns, or all small arms?"

"Bigger than a SAW?" she asked.

43

"Yeah, RPGs, grenades, mortars or heavy machine guns like .50 cals?"

She shivered.

"No, just guns."

That made me think of my KSG, and I wondered where my old friend had gone. Probably in a weapons locker somewhere, taken by the DHS. I nodded to her and kept going slowly. The figure saw us and waved. I waved back, and he started walking our way.

"That's probably him," I said.

"I think it is," Courtney said. "Looks like the guy who came upstairs to check on Steve a few times and talk about stuff."

The man's uniform wasn't clean and spit shined like the other deputies I'd seen, and there was a dried fleck of blood on his collar. He didn't look like he had been shot, so it must have been from someone else, I reasoned.

"Daniel Wright?" I asked.

"That's me. You're Dick and Courtney?" He offered me his hand.

I shook and nodded.

"Yeah, Steve asked me to talk to you. See if I can think of some ways of setting up more defensive measures."

He gave me a long look and then nodded. "Let's find somewhere in the shade, and I'll sketch things out for you."

* * *

THE DEVIL'S DUE

The farmhouse, barn, and wells were in the front third of a forty-acre parcel. It was planted in hay and Sorghum currently, and was almost utterly flat. Much of the surrounding land was as well, which could be a double-edged sword. We could see them coming from a long way off, but they could rain in shells from a long way off. Truth be told, that was my biggest worry, them finding our range and dropping artillery on us from afar. It'd be tough to miss, depending on if they had the right equipment and experience. If they had NATO troops with them, I didn't doubt they'd have the experience.

So, instead of seeing how to fortify it, I started looking at how to booby trap the ways in and out. Would they roll straight up the road again, or come across the country? I was worn out from the walk and still weak from my ordeal, so I headed upstairs to rest, sleep, and consider the problem before me. Before laying down, I looked out of the windows. The view was almost breathtaking: food, glorious food, planted as far as the eye could see. Corn, grains, grass for livestock—if there were any left in the area— and probably no way to harvest any of it.

That was what burned me. Why were they interring people at the camps, when they could have them out here, helping and building a community? What kind of work were they forcing them to do, besides gardening and clean up? Courtney had mentioned something about electrical components, but the expectations for the workers was very hard to meet, and it'd resulted in some harsh punishments. The more I heard about the camp, the more

BOYD CRAVEN

I wanted to bust it wide open.

From what I'd found out during my talk with Wright, the camp had forty DHS goons there full-time. The sheriffs had made up thirty-five men, for an internal police force before they'd left with their families, and they guessed there were at least two hundred citizens left behind. What we didn't know, was the numbers of the NATO force that had swept in to support them.

"So you have a plan?" Courtney asked, watching me from the doorway.

"Kill them, run them off. Haven't worked the details out yet. Just a rough outline."

"Tell me," she said.

I walked over and sat on the edge of the bed, and she joined me, plopping into the chair close to the bed.

"Two parts. Booby trap any entrances and exits they might use, or make it impassable for their heavy vehicles. The second part, sabotage their trucks and supply chain. Then, depending on what fate forces us to do, we'll either defend here, or we'll try to push them out first. The advantage is theirs, unless we come up with some nasty surprises."

I turned as I heard footsteps and saw Mel standing in the doorway. I smiled and motioned for her to come in.

"My dad's sleeping again. Mom was wondering what you thought?"

"Come in and sit down, I'll fill you in."

I told her what I'd started telling Courtney so far.

46

THE DEVIL'S DUE

"So, like you did at the trap house in Chicago?" she asked.

"Trap house?" Courtney asked.

"You weren't with us yet," Mel explained. "Dick rigged this apartment building to blow up, tricked the bad guys inside. Locked them in, rode a slide out of it, and blew it up before they could come out."

"What?!" Courtney looked at me with wide eyes.

"It wasn't as much fun as she's making out. But yeah, it was designed to get them all inside, draw them into one spot, then pick them off or slow them down one by one, and commence termination procedures."

"You blew them up?" Courtney asked.

"Well, yeah. This is farm country. And unless we're in an organic farming community, all the materials I need are right here."

"But can it go through the armor of those Hummers?" Courtney asked.

"If I can flip it, it won't matter much. It'll be unable to function. I thought I heard only a couple of vehicles were armored, though."

"We don't know what the NATO people have," Mel reminded me.

"That's true, but I doubt they're driving a ton of troop carriers with a turret."

"One of them had a big gun on a turret," Mel said.

"Yeah, and when we find something like that, we'll have to take it out quick before—"

* * *

"I told him he needed to rest," I could hear Doc's voice as an acrid smell assaulted my nose.

Smelling salts. I opened my eyes to see several people hovering over me.

"Hey," I said, pulling myself into a sitting position.

"You're either the most stubborn man alive, or one of the most ignorant," Doc said, a little red-faced.

I noticed his hands were shaking and he was huffing like he was out of breath.

"Did you run over here?" I asked him.

"Yes, I had to stop my lunch and run—"

"Doc," I said softly, "you'll work yourself into a heart attack. You're more important around here than I am. Please remember that."

I could see Jamie at the outer edges of the throng of people with Mel kneeling next to Courtney, who was sitting Indian style on the floor next to me. The rest consisted of Wright and a few deputies, probably responding to the call as if it were everyday America and they were doubling as medics, too.

"I'm not going to let an idiot like you die after I used all that medicine on getting you better. Steve says you're to be… I mean…" the doc sputtered. "They need you to help them… to set up…"

"I know, Doc," I said, throwing him a lifeline.

"They need him for what?" a red-faced deputy asked, probably in his mid-twenties.

"To teach us how to defend against the government agents," Soams told him.

"That's stupid," he said. "Why would we need an

old junky? If we have the equipment and manpower to raid a government camp to rescue him, we can definitely take care of ourselves here."

"It's not that easy," I told him. "Mortars or field artillery can take this entire farm out from miles away. They could send an armored column that will just drive through your fences and small arms fire. Unless you have heavy weapons and explosives, you don't have much of a chance."

"Hey," Mel said softly, "Dick's pretty good at this stuff, Scott."

"Come on, kid, stay out of it. You don't know what you're talking about," Scott said. Evidently, he was somebody that the O'Sullivans knew.

Jamie was giving him a pointed look, but he wasn't getting the message.

"I know more than you do," she spat back.

"Listen kid—"

"Scott, is it?" I asked, standing up. "Maybe you don't need me. But unless you've ever served, you don't have the training to take on military forces."

"We took on those DHS goons, killed them, and broke you out. I just don't understand why Steve and Doc wasted medicine on you. You got yourself hooked on the crack, and I'm sick of people wasting resources. You'd be dead, if Doc hadn't used a ton of stuff up. Those were medicines that we can't just go to the pharmacy and refill."

Several deputies stepped back as I flexed my shoulders, making a fist and feeling my tendons pop.

"You didn't take on military forces," I told him.

49

BOYD CRAVEN

"You took on hastily trained cops. Hell, I think even sheriff's deputies have less training than the DHS goons, they just have better equipment—"

"Better training than us?" he interrupted. "I spent four years in college and then went through the academy training to get to where I am. I'm not going to listen to a washed out crackhead—"

His words turned into a garble as I popped him in his Adam's apple, pulling the rabbit punch, so it wasn't a lethal one that crushed his windpipe. As he leaned forward, I helped his forehead find my knee that was rising. The contact sent a bolt of pain through my knee, but he crumpled onto his side, a nice red mark covering half of his face. My whole body shook in anger at the asshole's words. I didn't need to be a super soldier to realize that he wouldn't have been able to keep up with the job of law enforcement anywhere besides Podunk, Nebraska. He wasn't hard enough.

"Yes, better training than you guys," I said to the room at large, that had been stunned into silence. "I've got a masters in History, and almost seventeen years of combat experience. I've been to places that you can't find on a map, and I've killed people that I'm not allowed to even talk about. If you folks don't want my help, then you all can go fuck yourselves, but I'm going to make sure my daughter is safe."

Everyone looked at me and then around the room pointedly. Mel walked up and took my hand; it was still clenched into a fist at my side. Slowly, she made me open my hand and I felt myself calming. Doc knelt next to Scott, checking him for a pulse. I knew he'd find one. I'd just knocked him silly, so he didn't piss me off enough to cause me to have to kill him and make an example of him.

"Dick, it's ok," she told me, smiling weakly.

"It's ok, Maggs, I won't run out on you here."

"Who's Maggs?" Beth said, coming out of the kitchen and pausing at the sight of Scott laying on the floor.

"My daughter, Maggie…" I said, the anger leaving me swiftly.

Jamie looked at me, pity in her eyes. That puzzled me, and I took Maggie's hand. She gave me a squeeze back, and I turned to look at her. That was when I realized it was Mel.

"Oh, I thought you were talking about Mel there," Beth said. "What happened to him?" She pointed to Scott, who was starting to come around.

I let go of Magg—Mel's hand.

"He thought he had better training and that I was an oxygen thief. I let him test out his theory."

"You sucker punched him," Doc said angrily, holding a capsule of smelling salts under Scott's nose, much as he'd done with me.

"Well, yeah. He's in his early twenties. I'm not going to fight him fair. That's a good way to get hurt or get dead. See, that's why none of you are probably going to enjoy what I have to say. None of you cops probably have all the training you'd need… and we're not just going against DHS goons. It sounds like there's a NATO team now to reinforce them. Steve as much said so," I said, pointing up.

Now that the action was over, the adrenaline

was starting to leave me, showing me how weak I still was. It had only partially masked the weakness, shakes, and wobbles. I'd done too much, too fast, and I was paying the price. I'd be lucky, if I could do more than go back to bed for the day.

"So, you beat on him to make a point?" Beth asked, incredulous.

"No, I did it because he never would have believed me otherwise. They say you can't train an old dog. Well, you can, you just have to work with it more. You also can't train a young pup to listen when he's too headstrong, unless you beat it until it recognizes the alpha."

"You're crazy," one of the deputies said. "A schizo-junky, military-trained killer. I don't know who's scarier, you or the DHS."

He walked out, and after a couple of seconds, so did the rest of the deputies. Doc was helping Scott to his feet, shooting me an angry look before walking out. I walked to the windows, using the ledge to steady myself as they walked to the barn. The sliding side door was open, and although I couldn't make out everything inside, I could see movement. They had to have had bedding set up inside there, or in the entrance to the bunker.

"Dick," Jamie said from across the room, "I tried to cover for you before. I kind of think the cat's out of the bag."

"What do you mean?" I asked.

"When you get angry or stressed, you lose your grip. You go off the handle and hurt people. You get Mel confused with Maggie. I tried to keep that part of you secret from everyone, but they're right. You are a scary man… but I know you're a good one. They don't. You just made a point to everyone that they don't have enough training… but you also showed them that you're unstable and that nobody on either side of the fence is safe."

Shit.

Mel gave me a quick side hug and went outside, after grabbing a sidearm and putting it in a holster she'd been wearing on her belt.

"Oh, that's what that was about?" Beth asked, startling us all.

I had forgotten she was still in the room.

"Pretty much," Courtney said, moving to sit at the couch.

"So, you're off your meds or something?" Beth asked me.

"I don't even know what meds I need, Beth," I said, giving her a weak smile.

"Well, if you're half dead and you can do that," she said, pointing out the door, "then maybe they should listen. Maybe they could learn something from you."

I thought on that and nodded. "Jamie, Mel, Luis and Courtney all knew the shape I was in. They didn't mention my issues, probably to make it easier on you folks. I just wish I hadn't—"

"Dick, don't blame yourself for everything," Courtney interjected.

"But it's my fault that Luis is dead, and those men have no idea what the other side is capable of. I mean…"

BOYD CRAVEN

"Dick," Jamie cut in, "Luis wasn't your fault," she paused as Courtney started to sob softly. "The people who died here were not your fault. Is that what's got you so pissy?"

Partly. No, you are. Shit, I couldn't say that. "I lost my shit, I'm sorry." I didn't know what else to say.

"Dick, I told you, not everything is your fault," Courtney said, wiping at her eyes.

I heard a thump and a groan from the stairwell and saw that Steve had made it all the way down, except for the last three steps where he'd sat, his bad leg bandaged and lying straight out in front of him. Had he seen it all, too?

"I don't appreciate you manhandling my men," Steve growled, "but you're right. We're not ready to handle them. Law Enforcement training is usually… less lethal than how the media portrayed us. We don't have tactics and training on repelling armored vehicles and people using military strategies. What do you think of our situation here at the farm?"

I considered that carefully before answering.

"Unless we get proactive about defense, we're out of luck."

He nodded, and then stood.

"Dad, Doc said you couldn't be up for another couple of days!" Mel said, running over to him.

"I don't know how much time we have until they come back, kiddo. Might as well help get things ready, or at least deal with some of the younger men who're unruly," he said, shooting a glance at me, and then made a 'come here' gesture to Jamie.

THE DEVIL'S DUE

She went over and he whispered something to her. She nodded and put an arm under his shoulder and helped him walk out to the porch.

"You still need some rest and food," Beth said, coming back out of the kitchen, this time with two sandwiches on a paper plate, and handed them to me.

"I know," I told her, "I just overdid it today."

I moved to the couch and offered one of them to Courtney, who just shook her head. Beth looked like she was winding up to say something, but I put up a hand and gave her a nod, as if to tell her I'd work on it. She turned and went back into the kitchen. Within moments, I could hear murmurs and the banging of pots and pans.

"Sorry about that," I told Courtney.

"What?" she asked.

"Popping that guy and putting him down. That might have put you in a bad spot, if they'd reacted badly."

"They wouldn't. You were just telling them the truth, as ugly as it was. He needed to know, even if the truth hurts."

"My knee hurts. Getting old sucks," I griped, biting into the sandwich.

Now, I'd never proposed to a woman because of her cooking, but having met Beth, I was quite tempted. Beth had somehow managed to make me the world's greatest BLT on sourdough. The bacon was crisp, the tomatoes fat and juicy. On top of all of it was grated cheese and a piece of crisp lettuce. The produce wasn't cold as if it had come from a fridge, but it was amazing nonetheless. I made a moan of pleasure and took another bite. I felt eyes on me, and I turned to see Courtney staring at the sandwich. She may have not felt hungry, but she could see what I had.

When I offered her the second sandwich again, she didn't hesitate. She dug in as if she'd not eaten in days. We sat in silence until we'd both finished.

"I don't know what to do," Courtney said suddenly. "I had the rest of my life planned out. I mean, Luis and I were going to..."

Her words trailed off, and I took the plate from her and set it on the ground. She leaned over and I hugged her hard. She'd been crying off and on since I'd woken up, and at that moment, I decided we were going to get payback, no matter what. Something I'd mentioned earlier, but now I really meant it. That's when I heard an air siren go off. Both of us bolted to our feet and ran for the door, forgetting everything.

"What is that?" Courtney asked me as we both got outside.

"The signal to get to the bunker in the barn," Sebastian said as both he and Beth came flying out.

I stepped back, letting them go, before turning and walking back to the racks where the guns were. I smiled when I saw a vest, very much like the one I used to have before I was captured. I put it on and shouldered the AR-15 I'd carried earlier. I looked over to see that Courtney was following suit, putting on a vest of her own. These were heavier than mine though, with trauma plates in both the front and back. Nice. She tucked the pistol that she'd had

THE DEVIL'S DUE

on her holster earlier into the left side of the vest, so she could get to it with a cross-draw. I did the same with a 1911 .45 Colt, before grabbing spare magazines for both the carbine and pistol.

"I don't see everyone running for the bunker," Courtney said, looking out the door.

"Let's go, it looks like someone's at the gate," I told her, moving to head out.

CHAPTER 5

I stumbled, but Courtney and surprisingly, Doc were there to catch me before I ate dirt.

"Dick, dammit, you're not in any kind of shape to be doing this," Courtney gasped as she shouldered part of my weight.

Doc was similarly burdened, but he was an elderly man and he stumbled. I pulled him close to me and it was a miracle that all three of us didn't go over. Finally, I decided to go slower, instead of tripping and breaking bones. I felt a hand grab the back of my belt and saw Courtney bearing down.

"All right, you good now?" she asked.

"Yeah," I told her.

"Damned fool," Doc spat, "you should be headed for the bunker!"

"Wright's at the gate," I said, stopping. "Civilian

trucks are parked on the other side."

"How many men?" Courtney asked, giving my belt a tug.

"Dozen or so, armed with shotguns and rifles. All at ease. Looks like they are talking nice. Doc, you want to head to the bunker? You don't need to get involved in this."

"You ain't the only one with military experience," the old man paused, pulling up his shirt. Underneath was an old hog leg revolver, probably last used in WWII. I grinned evilly.

"Navy?" I asked him.

"About a thousand years ago. I can still shoot it, too. Now quit jacking an old man around. Let's get to that gate."

We moved, and as we got closer, I could hear their voices. They weren't quite yelling at each other across the chain link, but it was a close thing. Still, nobody had their guns at the ready position, so it hadn't turned violent yet. I could pick out Wright by his body language and the fact that he looked like an old cowboy in profile. Wide shoulders, narrow at the hip, with the broad hat of the Sheriff's Department on his head.

"…All we want is someplace to hold us over for the night," one of the men said, in a tone that was neither asking nor pleading.

"There's no room here. Farm's closed anyway. Just move on," Wright told him.

"It might just be better if y'all moved on," a familiar voice drawled.

I walked over and stood next to Wright and got a

good look at the hombres across the fence's big gate. I had been right about the numbers. Thirteen men stood there, armed with a hodgepodge of weapons. Most of them wore jeans and flannel shirts, with a few in sweat-stained t-shirts. A few old pickups had stopped in a line on the long driveway, sorghum planted on either side of the ruts.

"Maybe it'd be better off if you help folks. I mean, you're the cops. It's your job to protect and serve. We just need a place for tonight."

Then, for the second time, I realized something. I'd been used to seeing the sheriff's men, Steve included, being generally clean-shaven or at least with deliberate facial hair. These men not only were clean shaven, but their clothing was without dust or grime, and their haircuts were all close cropped.

"Where'd you come from?" I asked, startling the man next to me, "And what brings you to these parts?"

I felt Courtney give a little tug on my belt, letting me know she was still there to back me up, literally. The man next to me turned, and I saw the bruised and bloodied face of Scott from earlier. He blanched slightly when he realized he was standing beside me. I gave him a nod and turned to see what they had to say.

"We were just talking about that with the deputies here. Who the hell are you?" he snarled.

"The Avon lady," I replied.

The thing about playing a good bluff is, you have to be willing to actually go through with it. My measured response to the man, while standing shoul-

60

THE DEVIL'S DUE

der to shoulder with the deputies and I was in plain clothing, had to make them wonder who I was to these people.

"You in charge around here?" another man asked in a slightly accented voice.

It was supposed to sound Southern, but it was off. Everyone thinks they can pick out accents. What really throws things off is when a German first language speaker teaches a Russian first language speaker English. To make things worse, the garbled accent was trying to sound like a local dialect and it was making things all sorts of confusing. That's what I heard though: somebody who spoke English with a British accent, trying to sound like a Nashville country singer. And failing badly.

"Nope, I'm not," I said, almost jumping when a loud gunshot rang out from the farmhouse.

The shot hit the first truck in the grill. There was a shattering sound that echoed across the stillness, nearly drowning out the sound of the shot. Everyone on our side brought our guns up, hoping to back the play of whoever was at the house. There were only eight of us on this side, a handful of deputies, me, Courtney and Doc. The men on the other side had all hit the dirt when they heard the shot. The sound of fluid hitting the ground was the next thing I heard, and neon green fluid leaked out from the busted radiator of the first truck.

"Fucking sniper," a man from across the fence said, standing and brushing himself off.

Curiously enough, he hadn't tried hiding his accent. Definitely a British accent mixed with some-

BOYD CRAVEN

thing else. The other men stood as well, though none of them were raising their guns when they saw us ready for them.

"That's the man in charge back there," I said, hooking a thumb over my shoulder.

I let the carbine drop to my side on the sling and pulled the .45, racking the slide. "Drop your guns." I walked toward Wright, who was standing next to the chains that kept the gate shut.

"Yeah right," one of the too-clean-cut but now slightly dirty men spat. "We've got rights. Besides, all we were doing was—"

"Lying to me," I snapped coldly, raising the pistol so it was pointed in the man's face, from a distance of a few feet, separated by the chain link gate. "Open it," I said to Wright.

With one hand holding his gun, he managed to get the lock open. "Be careful," he whispered as I rolled it back a foot and stepped out.

The men on the other side backed up until the man I had my .45 trained on was standing in front of an inverted v shape with the other men behind him.

"Who are you boys with?" I asked, seeing heavy canvas tarps in the back three trucks' beds.

"We're just private citizens. We have the right not to be detained and if you take away those rights—"

I shot him when I was standing about three feet away, the top of his head disappearing in a spray of gore. The gunshot echoed and I heard murmuring and a struggle behind me.

"He can't do that," I heard somebody say, and

62

then a slapping noise.

I didn't turn to look, but instead held my pistol on the next closest man.

"You don't have rights here," I growled. "You're on private property. You drove up this driveway of your own free will. Now, who are you? Why are you here? AND IF YOU DON'T DROP YOUR FUCK-ING GUNS YOU'RE ALL DEAD!" The last came out as a scream of rage.

A couple of the men knelt down and placed their deer guns or shotguns on the ground in front of them, but most didn't.

"Stop him, Wright," I heard Scott say from behind me.

"Shut the fuck up," I heard Wright growl.

"One," I said, leveling the .45 in the next guy's right eye socket and pulling back the hammer.

"Two." He swallowed, his Adams apple bobbing up and down.

"Three." I pulled the trigger again and was hit again by the spray of pink mist.

Two things happened immediately, two gunshots rang out and I was punched in the back by a very large fist, twice, right in the main trauma plate, and the tarps on the trucks pushed themselves to the side as more men began boiling out. I fell and the world seemed to continue in slow motion. I fired as I fell, knowing I'd been shot. Several rounds hit the men closest to me, but as the slide on the .45 locked back, I hit my left side, pinning my arm. My whole world exploded in fresh agony.

I hadn't even been awake and conscious from

my drying out for a full day, and I'd already gotten into a fist fight, been shot, and had to execute two men. The ground exploded around me as somebody opened fire with what sounded like a demonic buzz saw. I heard screams from both side of the fence. Pulling my carbine close and trying to catch my breath, I started trying to fire one-handed toward the threats in front of us. A heavy punch in the gut sent me rolling back, almost senseless.

* * *

"We have to quit meeting like this, Doc," I said, peeling my eyelids open by sheer effort and the knowledge that I cheated the Reaper once again.

"You look like hammered shit," he said, a wry grin covering his blood-spattered face.

"What happened?" I asked, seeing that I was still where I'd fallen.

My entire body felt like one ginormous bruise. My chest hurt from both sides, and I started pulling at the Velcro straps on the vest so I could take deeper breaths.

"It was an ambush," Courtney said, also gore covered, thankfully none of which seemed to be coming from her or Doc. "They had a SAW in the last truck. It wasn't until whoever got the Barret up toward the house started firing on them, that they broke and ran."

"Any casualties?" I asked.

"Too damn many," Doc said, "some of which the two of us caused." He motioned to Courtney with the old hog leg revolver.

"What?" I pulled the vest off finally and rolled over so I could get a good look.

I could see that two of the three trucks were still there, large holes punched into the hood or the grill. Somebody up the hill had a Barrett .50 by the look and sound of it, a round that was known to be accurate to over a mile and able to crack the engine block of unprotected vehicles, or just tear a human in half, depending on the shot.

"Scott started pulling his gun, aiming it toward you. I tried to wrestle it away from him. That's how I got this," she said, pointing to an eye that was beginning to swell.

"Then I pulled my piece and tried to stop Scott from doing more. Instead, after you shot the second guy, he turned and fired at you. The blood's his," Doc said, pointing to his face. "A couple others trained their guns on us. I don't know what they were thinking, but we had to."

"I opened up on the ones who turned on us, going for headshots," Courtney said, "It wasn't until the SAW opened up on *all* of us and you were shot again, that the rest of the deputies turned and started firing back at the men. We cut down most of the first group, but the ones hiding in the trucks got away in the last one. Backed out before whoever was up on the hill back there shot the machine gunner."

"Wright's dead," Doc said. "He caught lead right in the beginning. He might have been able to stop the other guys from shooting at us. I know we had to have ended up killing some men who thought

I'd killed Scott for no reason. They were protecting their own. I was protecting ours." Doc's words burst out in an almost sob at the end.

Funny that he'd been pissed at me moments earlier for teaching the young deputy a lesson, and now he was on my side? The old man's chest started to hitch, and I heard a motor fire up. I looked back toward the barn and saw a quad approaching at a fast clip. On it were two men, one of which had a leg sticking out to the side at an awkward angle.

"Scott was bad news anyway," a deputy said, going over to stand by Doc. "But I saw it. I was about to draw on him after he punched the lady."

"Thanks for having our backs, Deputy…" Courtney paused, questioning. The blood spatter covered most of her face, and her lips were a dark red as a result of her trying to wipe her mouth clean and simply smearing it around.

"Crowder, rhymes with chowder. I just wish the others had been paying more attention. I know Wright had a look of shock on his face when Scott shot Dick, but it was probably cuz most of us have never had to fire our service weapons, and you just blasted those two away. I think, with what happened earlier, Scott snapped."

"Deputy Crowder, thank you," I said aloud and then to myself, *at least there's somebody who can explain the shit show to Steve who he might trust.*

"Pleasure," he said, tipping his hat slightly and turning to look at the approaching duo.

Make that trio, or more. Another motor had fired up and the Sheriff and another deputy pulled

THE DEVIL'S DUE

even to us, both red in the face. Neither of them were smiling and both pulled their guns on us.

"Drop the weapons," Steve said, holding a Barret Light .50.

"Not on your life," I told him, getting the .45 I'd dropped and regaining my feet.

I put a fresh mag in it and pulled the slide. I holstered the pistol and drew myself up to my full height, stretching and popping every sore tendon and bone in my body, noting where I hurt the worst. Everywhere. I kept my hands free of the weapons, but I could only guess what they had seen, and without context, what it must be perceived as.

"Doc, you, too," Steve said, motioning with the oversized rifle.

"Steve, you're going to listen to me here a minute. Thing is—"

The shot sounded like an explosion and the dirt erupted between me and Courtney. Doc was hit by flying dirt, but I had launched myself at the two cops, the instant the smoke came out the end of the Barret. Knowing I'd pay for it later, I hit both of them in a cross body block that sent the three of us over the side of the ATV. Steve tried to push back with the rifle, pushing me off, but I was using my weight and the arms and legs tangled up from the other deputy to keep him from taking another shot. Even though I was weak from everything, I was still heavier and I used my weight to advantage.

I drew the pistol at my hip, my ribs and chest on fire, and brought it down savagely. The deputy trying to untangle himself from Steve caught the pistol whip across the face. He went limp. Steve gave up on trying to push me off with the big rifle and started fumbling for his sidearm. I put the .45 against his right eye socket and he went very still.

"I'm tired of you assholes shooting and taking a swing me. If you weren't Mel's dad and Jamie's husband, I'd shoot you and leave you the fuck here!" I screamed with a rage I hadn't felt in a long, long time.

"You killed our men! What are you people, some kind of plant?! Double agents working for the DHS?!" he raged back, though his hands were no longer trying for a weapon.

Total exhaustion was about to make me pass out again, exhaustion and my overloaded pain receptors. I was glad when Courtney came over, pulled the Sheriff's pistol out of his holster and tossed it back. Then she helped me to my feet. I leaned against the quad with legs that were more Jell-O than bone and muscle.

"It's like Dick said," Courtney told him, "Your man shot first. Doc here put a slug through Scott's worthless brain after he tried to punch me out."

"It looked to me like he punched you because you were preventing him from stopping Dick from executing the men across the fence, without due process."

"There is no due process," Doc said. "It's Martial Law, and we're all in violation for even going around armed or breaking out from the FEMA camp. Have you forgotten that?"

Steve turned and looked at the doctor. "Soams,

what the hell, man? What happened?

"Dick," he said, nodding at me, "saw something was off. He was trying to prevent the ambush. He gave the men a chance to disarm, but they refused. They're not even Americans."

"You noticed that too, Doc?" I asked, gasping for breath.

Doc nodded and a look of shock replaced Steve's indignation as the second quad pulled up. Both of them had guns drawn, but weren't aiming at anybody.

"Sheriff? Steve?" one of the men asked, looking bewildered.

"It's ok, guys. Stand down. We've got to sort this mess out, and we don't need any more friendly fire." Steve's voice was soft, commanding, even after I'd taken both him and his man off the quad.

I offered my hand to Steve, who pulled himself up with one leg. The other he moved stiffly, from more than just the bandages that wrapped it. I pointed to a spot on his leg where blood was starting to seep through the gauze.

"Yer leaking, Sheriff," I said.

"Well shit, must have popped a stitch," he said, the color draining out of his cheeks as he surveyed the scene.

I took a chance to look around. The first group of men hadn't been entirely mowed down. Seven of them lay lifeless. On our side, it was bad. Really bad. Of the deputies, four of them were down hard: Wright, Scott, and two others that I'd never learned the names of. Of them all, only Crowder remained, plus, Doc, Courtney and I.

"What…" the deputy I'd pistol whipped, moaned and rolled over, throwing up.

"Great, another concussion to treat. It's bad enough when our own assholes are trying to kill us," Doc raged.

"What happened?" Steve asked me.

"We came up for the last half. Wright was telling them to head out. They said they wanted in, just for the night, and they weren't taking no for an answer."

"But you saw something off?" he asked, as another deputy helped Doc get the one I'd pistol whipped to his feet.

Steve joined me, sitting on the back of the quad to get the weight off his bum leg.

"Yeah, they were all clean cut, and clean. Their clothing wasn't dirty, and they looked like they were right out of a Marlboro commercial."

"They don't advertise tobacco on TV anymore, it's illegal," a young deputy interjected.

"They did when you were nursing on your mommas titties, now shut up," I replied blandly.

He gave me an angry look and I stared at him a while, till he turned away.

"As I was saying, I started to talk to them. I noticed one of the guys had a slight accent and I remembered when Jamie had tried to contact you on the road… it wasn't the same voice, but the same accented English."

"Yeah, that's the NATO regiment," Steve said.

I nodded, it made sense. "So I had Wright open the gate. The rest of the men were backing off to give

70

THE DEVIL'S DUE

themselves more space to bring their guns to arms when you blew the front out of the first truck. Nice shot, by the way."

"Thanks," Steve said with a half-hearted smile.

"That's when we got the complete drop on them. The guy I had dead to rights kept crying about his rights, and I heard Scott behind me start some ruckus. I didn't know it, but he'd cuffed Courtney. I counted the man down to disarm and he never took me serious till his head was turned into pink mist. The second guy I did the same way, thinking after that, they would be easy to manage. That's when I was shot in the back." I turned and spit toward Scott's body. "Oxygen thief. And that's when they sprang the trap. You saw the rest, I think?"

"They opened up with a SAW, you caught more lead and fell. Then I saw Doc blow Scott's brains apart, and when the others tried to disarm him, your lady friend started firing on my own men."

"They weren't trying to disarm us," Courtney said pointedly. "You keep forgetting; this isn't police action out here. They were going to kill us. They were probably good men, but if I have to choose between me and a stranger, the stranger is going to lose every time. They never should have tried shooting Doc and me. Besides, it would have been better to have four or five more guns on the men who attacked us, instead of your men trying to kill us."

Courtney was mad, and although some of her anger was righteous, I also knew it had a ton of mitigating factors as well. Still, I knew she could use that anger to put off some of the pain of losing Luis such

71

a short time ago.

"Yeah, that was a cluster," Steve admitted after a long pause.

"Ya think?" Doc asked.

The phrase coming out of an eighty-three-year-old man's mouth, just as snarky as Maggie had been when I'd last seen her in the flesh, caught me funny. I started chuckling and pretty soon Courtney joined in. The deputies just stood there slack jawed, looking at us, obviously finding no humor in the apocalypse.

"Hey, if they can't take a joke, fuck 'em," Doc said angrily.

That more than anything, made everyone else bust up.

CHAPTER
6

I spent a good portion of a week healing up and staying out of sight. The men we'd killed, the cops, had family at the compound. Courtney and I stayed in the room upstairs and out of the public eye. It was just easier that way. At first, we'd thought we were going to get lynched at the general meeting that Steve had held after the attack, but he was more than just a cop. The sheriff was a politician of sorts, and was practiced in the art of well… politics. He had the gift of gab. Although he did not like our final solution and how everything had panned out, he understood that under fire, we'd had no other choice. I'd just been bastard lucky to have been wearing one of the vests, otherwise I would have been dead five times over.

I'd been hit in the back twice and stitched three

times by the SAW in the front. Usual trauma plates would have probably cracked or shattered under the onslaught of the SAW's ammunition, but Steve had ordered some 10x12" plates from a company in Florida that had promised that they would stop up to a .350 WinMag round. Still, I needed a week. I'd ended up purple from the nipples to my belly button on the front, and my back was one solid bruise in the shape of the plate, from getting hit at close range. Part of me wondered if that had been Scott's plan all along, to just knock me down, or had he been trying to kill me?

Those were the pleasant thoughts that I dealt with on a day to day basis, as I played endless hands of cards with Courtney, when I wasn't talking strategy with Steve and gobbling Tylenol. I'd given him a list of items to pick up, to try to make the place more defensible, and he'd actually smiled at the items. He'd been able to source all of it easily, even the materials to make thermite. How easy it was to get the stuff had been a surprise to me at first, but he'd pointed out that it was farming country, and that made it easy to source.

"You seem like you're a thousand miles away," Mel said, walking into the room.

I'd been sitting in the chair, thinking again. I knew we needed to bring the fight to them, but I wasn't sure where they were yet, and I was still shaky. A lot of naps, a lot of rest, and food had all helped. I was almost back on my feet, but every additional day that I could rest up, helped a lot.

"Sort of," I told her. "Just thinking about everything. About making it safe for me to leave you here at the farm, so I can go home to Mary and Maggie."

"Do you think that's going to happen soon?"

I nodded. "I'll hate to go, but I think we're going to wrap things up here soon, for better or worse."

"I hope it's for the better…"

I'd been sharing the room with Courtney; she hadn't wanted to be alone and was having horrible nightmares, just like me. Either of us or both of us could have used the bunks in the basement or the bunker, but we hadn't wanted to mix with the general population of the farm because of the bad feelings that still lingered… so other than washing the bedding of the bed I'd detoxed in, we'd stayed in the room. The big plus was it had its own bathroom, a luxury of luxuries, and the shower turned off.

"Listen, it would mean a lot to me and Mom if you would come down for dinner tonight. I know that things aren't the best with everyone right now, but… I kind of miss you two. I know Mom does, too."

That made me almost turn crimson. Jamie missed me? That was news to me. She'd been avoiding me as much as I'd been avoiding her. For me, it was about me letting her go. I hadn't even realized I'd started falling for her until Courtney had pointed it out. Dealing with the shame and guilt was one thing, but when I'd kissed her, it had seemed like everything was all right in the world. Part of me knew that it'd been the smack talking, or at least some of it, but she'd kissed me back. Then her husband had gotten involved and the rest, as we say, was finito.

BOYD CRAVEN

"I'll talk to Courtney. If I can talk her into it, we'll be down."

"Good, dinner is at six tonight, in about two hours." She walked over and gave me an impulsive hug.

I hugged her back, smiling. Since coming to the farm, things had been stiff, impersonal. Part of it was because of Steve and Jamie and my hang-ups, the other was because of everything that had gone down. That was probably why nobody had objected to me and Courtney bunking in the same room. We'd stayed out of sight, both of us in mourning and fighting our own demons.

"Good, I'll see you then, I hope," I said, and let her go.

Like no other fifteen going on sixteen-year-old, she all but skipped out of the room, closing the door behind her. The bathroom door opened a crack and a billow of steamy air filled the already muggy bedroom.

"Dick, can you come here a second?" Courtney asked.

"Sure," I said, rising and heading toward the bathroom.

I knew she'd have her robe on. While we'd all lived and traveled together, modesty had been somewhat thrown out the window; that happens, and it wasn't something that was weird between all of us. But now that we were back in a house and small community, certain protocols were to be followed. Even though we had an unusual arrangement in sharing space, it was honored.

76

THE DEVIL'S DUE

Courtney was standing on the tiled floor, wiping the mirror with a hand towel. The sink was littered with dry corn silk colored hair. She'd cut it almost to her shoulders and had probably showered afterward.

"Is this straight?" she asked.

I ran my hand along the back of her hair. She'd towel dried it, but it was still damp. I grabbed a brush off the sink and started running it through her hair, to pull it down and see how good of a job she'd done trimming it up.

"You know, Jamie is the hair cutter person," I told her.

She let out a small moan. "Do that for a second," she said, leaning back slightly as I kept running the brush through and holding the ends with my free hand.

I put the brush down and got the scissors, taking care of a few spots in the back that she couldn't have seen. I started brushing it back out, wondering why she hadn't asked Jamie to cut her hair, and decided to chalk it up to not wanting to be harassed by the rest of the small community. Another moan escaped her lips and she backed up, pressing herself into me. I dropped the brush and backed up. She closed the distance faster than I'd moved away and pinned me in the doorjamb. To move would have meant brushing her with my body, but she reached back with her hands, caressing my cheek.

She turned and my breath hitched as I caught the scent of Mary's freshly washed body. Soap, shampoo, and a slight fragrance that could only be the body spray that she knew drove me crazy. She dropped the robe and pushed me gently, directing me, until the back of my knees hit the bed. I fell backwards, pulling her on top of me.

"No talking," Mary told me as she kissed me, her hands working at my belt and then the top button of my pants, pulling them off.

Oh shit, I knew my return home was going to be rocky, but I'd never expected to be greeted by my wife like—

The door banged open and a woman let out a surprised shriek and then the door slammed shut again, but not before I'd seen Jamie's face. Full of hurt, shock, embarrassment. I looked up and saw Courtney, not Mary, her own face looking surprised, ashamed.

"Oh shit," I said, rolling her off of me so I could get up.

"Dick, please," Courtney said, pulling at me.

That stopped me. The way she'd asked. The raw pain. Instead of hopping off the bed I stopped, and looked into her eyes, both of us on our sides now. Difference was, I was still more or less clothed and I forced my eyes to only look at her face.

"I'm sorry, I thought you were Mary," I said, feeling the tears forming.

"I just wanted to be close to somebody," Courtney said starting to sob. "There's something wrong with me. When Luis died, something broke. I need to be needed, Dick," and then she buried her head in my chest, crying.

Something inside of me broke loose, and I start-

THE DEVIL'S DUE

ed to cry as well. I knew I should have gone after Jamie, explained the situation, but I couldn't leave Courtney like this. I even managed to get my britches more or less back in place. At some point, one of us must have pulled the afghan up, because I was suddenly warm and wrapped in her arms. We fell asleep, nose to nose, so intertwined in our grief that we lost all sense of time.

* * *

I recognized this place. We were all standing in a row, waiting for the preacher to say the final words. The military funeral had been skipped and instead, a smaller one in the hometown had been opted for. I was standing beside Mike, and he and James were standing on either side of Mary and Maggie, who were both dressed in black, black lace veils covering their faces.

"This must be a memory, a dream?" I asked myself, unable to move, to only watch.

Both Mike and James were dead, one by my hand, one by my hand not being where it should have been. James turned and smiled at me, his teeth filed to points. I shivered, despite the realization that this wasn't real.

"Dearly beloved, we are gathered here to honor…" The priest's words weren't right, and I barely listened, as I tried to catch the features of Mary and Maggie. Both were older than I remembered and Maggie had grown both taller and matured. My heart ached at seeing them, and I was having a hard time figuring out if this was some sort of amalgam of a dream, part fact, part fiction... and then we were moving.

"You're going to love this," James said, shooting me a toothy grin as we lined up to see the casket before it closed.

"Leave him alone," Mike told the cannibal. "You're going to be fine," he told me, giving James a reproachful look.

My heart raced as I waited my turn. Every step closer to the casket was a step closer to Mary and Maggie. I didn't understand why they were up front in the family section of a funeral, but this was a dream, and it'd been years since I'd seen the two of them. One by one, the people in front of us shuffled, waiting their turn to talk to the ladies, to speak words to whomever was in the casket. Then Mike's turn was up. He turned and gave me a smile.

"It's going to be ok," he told me.

I waited, but he followed suit just like everyone else. It was going to be ok? What was going on here?

"This is going to kill you," James said, his voice phlegmy, and he laughed the crazy laugh I'd remembered in my nightmares. Then it was my turn.

I stepped up to the casket and looked down.

One of my many conversations with Skinner haunted me suddenly.

"Who are you?"

"Dick Pershing," I answered.

"Wrong. Why did you murder Ben's family?"

"I've never committed murder," I answered truthfully.

THE DEVIL'S DUE

"Who are you?" he repeated.

"Dick Pershing."

"Dick Pershing is dead!" Spittle flew from his mouth, and he swung an emaciated hand at me.

I looked down into the coffin and saw myself lying there. I looked up to see Maggie's eyes, and they were full of tears. Mary looked at me with sorrow in her eyes, her soul damaged by what had happened.

I tried to move toward them. "I don't understand—"

* * *

The knocking at the door woke me up.

"Dick, dinner time," Mel's voice chirped.

Jamie must not have told Mel, I thought, pulling the blanket back. Courtney was bare from head to toe and I quickly pulled the covers back over her. She curled up as I did that, pulling a pillow close to her stomach before snoring softly, stopping, then rolling over again.

"Hey, you coming to dinner?" I asked her.

"Dinner?" she asked thickly. "Yeah, give me a minute."

"We'll be right there," I told Mel through the door.

"Okay!" I heard her walking down the stairs.

"Dick?"

I turned and Courtney was standing beside the bed, one hand over her head stretching. I tried not to stare, but she was yawning and every muscle in her body pulled taut as she shivered a moment.

"Yeah?" the words barely escaped my mouth as I tried to look away, at my feet, at the ceiling.

"I'm sorry," she said as I finally turned around.

"How come?" I asked her, facing the corner.

She walked over, wrapping her arms around my back and squeezed me.

"For what I did, what almost happened. I was feeling down and I think I needed a cry more than I needed a… you know. I'm… listen, I'm not good at this. Don't make me say it."

"I'm not upset at you," I told her, "that wouldn't be fair to either of us."

"No, but what I did wasn't fair to you. I thought… I mean… I feel bad for saying this, but for half a second, I thought that if I could have you, even for a moment, I could try to forget Luis."

That was a sobering thought and I realized that I had underestimated the depths of her pain. She was still in love with him, and was ready to tarnish his memory to just get over him, even if it brought on the guilt. What made it worse was my mind had slipped, and I'd thought she was Mary. I would have gone for it, right up until Jamie had—

"Oh shit," I said.

"What?"

I turned, and she had already pulled on a clean pair of panties, from a bag of clothing that the O'Sullivans had provided. The rest of her was bare so I started to look away, but she stepped into my vision.

"Please don't," I said. "I don't want to, I mean, I can't…"

THE DEVIL'S DUE

"Oh, yeah, sorry. In the museum where they kept us, our modesty, dignity, and sense of shame were the first things to go. Nudie time was an every day, all day thing. Sorry, Dick."

I looked away again and went on with my original thought. "When it was happening… Jamie walked in."

"Oh god, I thought it was Mel. Figured I'd scarred the kid for life. How did she react?"

She walked back into my sight, a loose pair of gym shorts and a plain white t-shirt on. Her blonde hair was disheveled from drying weird, but other than that, she looked like an ordinary young adult lady who was a stunning beauty. With bedhead. I shook my head to clear that thought, and every other one I had still floating in the reptilian brain of mine.

"She looked hurt. Pissed."

"Damn."

"Yeah, I don't need any more problems here for us," I said.

"No, it's kind of like I thought," Courtney said more to herself than me and walked toward the window, looking out.

I could see the reflection of her face, her eyes staring out into the blank slate that was the new world around us.

"What's that?"

"Nothing," she said. "You mentioned dinner? How's my hair?"

"Your hair is fine, that's what got us into… uh…"

"Yeah… Dick, don't take this the wrong way, but

that's not going to happen again. I'm sorry that my meltdown led to… one of yours?"

"Good, I uh… we don't need that. I mean, we do, just not with each other, I mean… shit."

She wrapped her arms around me and squeezed again, then pushed me back. Hard. I almost hit the window.

"What the hell?"

"Just making sure you weren't getting too comfortable. This isn't a sob-fest any more. We need to gut up and move on with shit. Especially when we head to Arkansas."

"I thought you were going to break off and go to Texas?" I asked her.

"Yeah, well… Arkansas is on the way. You weren't going to kick me to the curb early, were you?" The snarky, fierce woman was re-asserting herself in the contours of her face. The fire in her eyes that had been missing the past week was back. I knew what she was doing was an act, but maybe it was a necessary lie to fake happiness and the tough attitude until it was real. Maybe that would work. I'd heard the phrase 'fake it till you make it' enough that there must be some truth to it somewhere. Besides, would she really want to go to Texas without Luis?

"I wouldn't kick you to the curb, you've been to Hell and back with me."

"And don't you forget it," she said, opening the bedroom door.

Feeling even more confused than I had several hours ago, I followed.

84

CHAPTER
7

I sat across from Courtney, next to Mel. With as many people they had at the farm, the table was put up and taken down apparently, and Beth hadn't been kidding, people ate in shifts. I wondered when the woman ever slept, she seemed to be constantly filling or refilling empty places on the table with food. It was a feast. It was more than I'd ever expected, and I was immediately suspicious of Steve's easygoing manner. He'd always been tense and wary around me, but suddenly he was cracking jokes and treating me like a long lost friend.

What the hell. Fake it till I make… Naw.

Courtney was laughing with half a mouthful of food as one of the deputies was telling stories about some of his most ridiculous arrests, and I must admit, the one about the man who broke into his neighbor's house because he'd belatedly found out he had no TP, was only compounded by the problem that he'd been caught with his pants down. Literally.

Mel was mostly soaking up the conversation, probably having grown up with many of the men as guests of her father. Jamie, on the other hand, picked at her food, moving it around the plate.

"Not hungry?" I asked her, ignoring the rest of the conversations going on around us.

"No," she said, so softly that I didn't hear it, I just saw her lips move.

"I'm sorry," I said, and let it go.

She looked to the left, toward the big window facing the front door. After years of living underground, I wanted to be outside a lot… but the reason I'd stayed in was because of some of the hard feelings over the dead cops caused by me and mine; yet none of that was evident today.

"More potatoes, Dick?" Mel asked, handing me a cast iron pot that weighed a ton.

"Just a little," I said, scooping them out and then tried to find an empty place at the table to put them down.

"There's nowhere to put this," I said, looking around.

"That's Beth's way of making sure it all gets eaten," Steve said with half a mouthful.

"Well, what do I do with it?"

"Pass it on," he said, eating half a homemade biscuit in one bite.

I handed it to my left, to the boisterous dep-

THE DEVIL'S DUE

uty. He took it and scooped then handed it on. I watched and as it made its way to Jamie, she just shook her head and it was passed behind her chair.

"So, why the feast?" I asked Steve.

"Remember the scouts you had me send out a couple of days ago?"

"Yeah, the ones to check out the camp."

"They just came back. The DHS at the camp is mobilizing. I don't know if they're going to be moving away, moving against us, or what's going on exactly. They are packing to move out in formation and the radio chatter has been confusing."

"So, there isn't anything we can use really? I mean, we can't get close enough to see more than that…"

"There's more. It appears that the NATO troops that fired on us, are there at the camp."

"That figures," Courtney spat. "I guess I know which way we're going first." She locked eyes with me.

I nodded. She'd have her justice and blow away as many of the murderous bastards as she could, and then maybe, just maybe, she could start healing.

"How about our list of materials?" I asked.

"I'm ahead of schedule. If they try to come in, I have enough ANFO to drop a sky scraper, all mixed and sealed in fuel drums. We're working on digging ambush points, placing charges, stuff like that."

I suddenly knew why he was in such a good mood. Despite things looking grim, the farm was getting ahead of the eight-ball for once, and getting things done while we still had options. I had thought that Steve was only half paying attention when I'd asked for a laundry list of supplies, but that hadn't been the case. He'd come through. All except for…

"And I got the stuff for the thermite," he said, smiling.

He'd got it.

"That's great. Magnesium Ribbon?" I asked.

His face fell. "No, actually I didn't. I heard we can use something else, though."

"As long as you have some sparklers around here, we're in good shape," I said with a smile.

"You going to teach us how to make it?" Mel asked.

"You little pyro." Her dad mussed up her hair. "A lot of us are going to learn how to do it. You're welcome to watch. We have some folks using the mortar and pestles that you asked about."

"Good deal. I'll build those after dinner then. Maybe in the early morning, me and Courtney can do a quick test of them."

"Oh, I want to see that! Mom, don't you want to see that?!" Mel asked, her voice excited.

It'd almost be infectious, her excitement, but Jamie just looked at her and nodded. Steve finally noticed his wife's dour mood and shot her a puzzled look. She met his gaze for a minute, looked at me and then turned back to the window.

"You can't watch where we're going to be testing it out, kiddo." I told her.

"Oh? Where's that?" Jamie asked, an edge to her

voice.

"On the hood of one of those APCs, if they're outside the fence."

The boisterous deputy and Steve started laughing like evil imps when they realized my plan simultaneously, and I gave them a grin. When I looked over to see Jamie, I met her gaze. She looked confused, hurt, and pissed. None of them were things that I wanted to see. I was torn and twisted in so many ways, and seeing her in pain only made the guilt I was feeling ratchet up.

"It's going to be fun," I said, looking at Courtney who was smiling at the thought of some payback. "Steve, if you could loan me a couple guys, some guns, and ammo, I'll leave about three am. I hope we can take out whatever big vehicles we can. If that doesn't look possible, I'll need intel on the camp. I want to put them on the defensive, until the preps here are ready."

"Sure, I'll have a couple guys come with you. What kind of load-out will they need?"

"Just strong backs and nerves of steel. Doesn't even have to be deputies."

"Doesn't have to be just men, either. That's sexist," Mel said and I snickered, despite myself.

"Well, if you think you can lug… oh never mind, kiddo. I know you can, but I doubt your dad would let you go."

"Yeah, kid, that ain't happening," Steve said, hugging her with one arm.

"I'm going to take a quick walk," I stood, and frowned when Courtney did as well. "No, it's ok,

BOYD CRAVEN

Courtney, I'm just going to the front porch. I need a little air to wake me up from all this wonderful food."

She nodded and sat back down. So much to do, so much planning. The days here were strange. Hot, hot, hot, during the daytime. Well, it should be, it was summer time. But it was the evenings that were to die for. Things cooled down, and there was a magical hour when the bugs didn't eat you alive. That was this very moment, and I wanted some time to make my peace with life.

The door opened and Jamie walked out, and leaned against the railing. For once, the porch was empty, except for the two of us.

"Jamie—"

"Stop." Her voice was so quiet that I struggled to hear it.

"About earlier—"

She put her hands over her eyes and shook her head. One hand fell down and it found its way into mine. I felt the moisture and looked up, seeing her tears falling silently.

"No, I get it, and I don't even know why it bothers me. I mean, I'm home and my family is back together again, but walking in on you and her—"

"I fell in love with you," I interrupted her.

Her head snapped around and she pulled both hands to her stomach in a knot.

"I didn't mean to," I continued. "I didn't even realize it was happening until the night I got the radio hooked up and you talked to Steve. I didn't know how prickly and grouchy it was making me.

90

THE DEVIL'S DUE

Courtney pointed it out, and I've been fighting it ever since. It was like once I found out, things made sense. It just made things worse for me. I'm sorry, I'm sorry I did that. Never once did I mean to hurt you."

"You… I…" her words trailed off and she just stood there, looking off in the distance.

"You have your family, your husband and a life. Somewhere out there, I have Mary and my daughter. I got turned around earlier, but nothing happened with Courtney. We were just two screwed up people who *almost* made a bad choice. And this thing I feel… I'm leaving, Jamie. I'm leaving soon to reclaim the life that I let slip through my fingers."

I was looking at the sun, setting over the waves of corn and grain, and I felt her hand on my arm.

"I… I'm kind of in the same boat," she said, "but when you're gone, it won't be so bad. I just can't… it hurts right now."

"I know. We spent a lot of time together. We've saved each other. It's a bond that nobody else can share. But it's a bond created under extreme circumstances. You've got a life here, and mine's waiting for me to pick up the threads." The words tasted like ashes in my mouth, but I knew they were necessary.

"I know," Jamie told me, pulling a tissue out of her pocket and blowing her nose. "I just saw that, and I hadn't realized it myself. Kind of like what you felt when I called Steve."

The stab of the little green monster; yes, yes, I knew it well.

91

"I know. But Courtney and I won't ever be a thing. I had a flashback, and for a moment, I thought I was in Mary's parents' farmhouse, with Mary."

"How do you keep things together? You're one of the most broken human beings I've ever met, and also the toughest one mentally. I don't understand how you can still be standing here sometimes."

"I don't know either. Lately, I've been dreaming of Skinner, of him telling me that I'm dead. They have record of me dying. I'm not dead, but my mind is working on something. Maybe the dreams are so much mental diarrhea, that it's how my mind copes."

"Your feelings, are they mental diarrhea?" she asked, half smiling.

I knew what she meant, and it was a tricky question to answer. I took a deep breath.

"No, I just feel sorry that my feelings made things rough on you. What I feel doesn't matter. I'm moving on, you know that. I just hope I didn't hurt you and Mel by wearing my heart on my sleeve."

"No." She hugged me. "Just come back safe tomorrow. I want to make sure that you make it to Arkansas. I want you to find your Mary and Maggie."

I let her go and used a thumb to wipe away the last tear running down her cheek.

"I do, too. That's why I wish I would have hid how I felt better."

"No, one thing you don't do is hide your feelings. If you had tried, you would have exploded.

92

THE DEVIL'S DUE

I'm going to rejoin the others. Beth has some apple pie coming up. You coming back in?"

"In a bit," I said, watching her give me a half wave as she went inside.

I sat on the steps and in a half a heartbeat, I heard heavy footsteps. I figured it was Courtney coming to give me a dig about Jamie, and was mentally preparing a defense against her antics when Steve sat down next to me.

"Steve," I said.

"Dick."

The silence stretched out, and I turned from my view of the sunset to see him struggling with words.

"I'm a lot of things, Dick. A county Sheriff, a farmer, a father, and a lousy husband. At first, I was almost glad when my wife walked in on you and Courtney. Almost."

Oh, shit.

"Thing is, I caught most of your conversation, because the other thing I am is a jealous bastard."

I waited for the punch. I'd leave myself open to it, I wouldn't even fight back. I deserved this.

"Thing is, I kind of understand where you're both coming from, and it's been eating away at me."

"You met someone?" I asked, a sudden flash of insight lighting up the shadowy, cobwebby corners of my brain.

"Yeah, I mean, Jamie and Mel were gone for months and months. I thought they were dead."

I let that sink in... Holy shitballs, Batman.

"Out of the blue, my wife is hauled into the FEMA camp we're helping to run, and it was like

BOYD CRAVEN

we were never apart. The love was still there. I can't thank you enough for bringing them back, but hearing you with Jamie just now... Shit..."

"You don't know what to do?"

"See, Frankie had been working for me for a couple of years. She was like a kid sister to me. I got her the gig with the department because she was my buddy's cousin, and she just needed a door opened..."

"And you two became close?" I asked.

"It was platonic for years. It was a month after I had started to believe Jamie to be dead that she found me. I had my service pistol in my mouth. She told me how she felt, how she had been feeling, and begged me not to do it. I wanted to, but suddenly I realized I wanted something else, too."

"To be needed?" I asked him, remembering Courtney's raw admission.

"It was more than that; I needed to be loved. I realized that part of me did have feelings for her, so we explored the relationship and it grew over time."

"Wait, where is Frankie now?"

He wiped his eyes and looked at the barn and pointed.

"Staying away from me. Kind of like the way you were avoiding Jamie for a while there. I thought you were doing that for me and I could see right through you... but just now... I feel bad I ever thought..."

"You're going to tell her?" I asked him suddenly.

"Yes, I have to. It's eating me up inside. Guilt, shame. I knew from the radio that Michigan was

94

basically a ruins. I didn't think they'd cross the country by foot—"

"And bike."

"And truck," he said with a sad grin, "but now I've got to sort this mess out and I have to come clean to my wife. I have to get over the fact that every facet about you that I hated from the start, is because I was in your shoes, literally. I just have to figure out how to tell—"

"You're going to stay with Jamie?" I asked him, hating myself for that question.

"Of course," he said. "It's not fair to Frankie, but I have to tell Jamie without screwing everything up for all of us. We're so close to having things safe here, but I can't keep this secret."

"What will you do about Frankie?" I asked him.

"Tell her the truth."

The door opened and I turned to see Mel coming out with two plates full of apple pie, so thick that the filling was oozing out the sides. It smelled heavenly.

"The truth about what?" she asked, handing plates to both of us.

"Grownup stuff," Steve said with a grunt.

"Dad, I'm sixteen in a month. How much more grownup can it be than what I've already seen?"

"Touché," he said, "still, it's personal."

"Oh…. Gotcha. When Danielle and Jeremy had 'personal' stuff to talk about, it was always sex. Those two would sneak away every time Dick wasn't watching. You two aren't having sex, are you?"

I snapped my head back and she grinned, despite turning slightly red in the face.

"What? They're grownups!" she said, a little indignant at the look I was giving her.

"They're just kids," I growled, adopting Steve's tone, "and me and your father aren't having sex together. With each other..."

"They're eighteen and nineteen," she said, ignoring how red in the face we both were getting. "What age is it ok to be a grown up nowadays?"

"Eighteen and nineteen is old enough, but you're fifteen and you don't even have a boyfriend," Steve told her. "Or at least if you do, I'd better not find out. It's been a few days since I shot somebody."

"Daaaaaaaaddddddddyyyyyyyyyyyy!" Mel went back inside.

"Is your daughter like that?" Steve asked me.

"I don't know. I haven't been around in a while. I hope so. You've got a good kid there, despite her sense of humor."

"Thanks. By the way, Dick..."

"Yeah?"

"You kind of look purty in this light," he said with a snicker.

He stood and went in the house, and I heard voices rise up, and him teasing Beth that her cooking was good enough to tempt Satan out of Hell. Giggles. Laughter. After a while, I ate the pie, but it had gone cold by the time I was done. I wasn't the only one with a heavy heart. We were all suffering to a degree here. Everyone but Mel. Jamie and me because of obvious reasons, Steve, Courtney. What a mess.

CHAPTER 8

The materials to make thermite can vary, but what had been procured was just about perfect for our needs. One of the farms had a small metal shop where the former owner had a metal lathe and a ton of aluminum shavings in a bin, waiting to be recycled. Also, in the shop was a lot of square steel tubing for making farm implements. The thing about the tubing was it wasn't treated, and it had rusted. It was from that and numerous other farm implements, that they'd collected the rust flakes. Both the rust and aluminum had been ground down as much as possible in a mortar and pestle, into a fine powder.

In fact, I hadn't counted on the particles being so fine. Many idle hands had taken turns turning both the rust and aluminum from big pieces into small pieces. Mel had told me that many of the ladies had been working nonstop at it, taking turns when Steve had told them what he thought I had in mind for it. In the barn, in one of the cupboards over Steve's tool bench, was a box of fireworks from when Mel was younger. A brick of sparklers had been sitting unused. It was almost too easy and perfect. I had at least five pounds of thermite material and I hoped it would be enough. If it wasn't, things were going to be interesting anyway.

"What do you want to hold the powder in?" Beth asked when I asked her to be in on it.

"Do you have metal coffee cans? Or the larger soup cans?" I asked.

"Big cans? You're kidding, right?"

"No, not at all."

"Well darn, those big number 10 cans are what Mr. O'Sullivan uses for his food storage. I could probably scare up several dozens of those."

"I think we'll need at least one, and at least three big soup cans about this size," I told her, showing her with my hands.

"Oh yeah, I got some that'll probably work."

The dinner dishes had been cleared and the pyrotechnics had been brought in. I was still stiff and sore, most of my body now a camouflage of colors, but I was ready for action.

"Grenade casing?" Steve asked.

"Yeah," I told him, "but we'll need some tin snips to trim the lids down some, too."

"Good thing I saved those lids then, isn't it?" Beth asked Steve, a smug smile on her face.

THE DEVIL'S DUE

"Yes, ma'am," he grinned back.

"How do you want the lids trimmed?" Steve asked.

"Just enough to fall inside of the container. Doesn't need to be far. We need to poke a hole in the top for the sparklers, too."

"Anything else?" he asked.

"A few books of matches for a timer," I told him.

He nodded and in a few minutes, Steve's men had everything at the table. Steve started trimming the lids and cut the wire handles off the sparklers, lining things up next to me. I was checking the mix on the thermite, trying to eyeball if it was 50/50 and decided that it probably was. It wasn't an exact science, but there were a lot of different varieties of thermite, and some were more useful for welding than what I was trying to do. The mix I had would be okay. I didn't want to make a bomb, just melt some stuff.

I used a canning funnel to pour scoops of the powder into each can, leaving an inch open at the top. I took one of the new lids and dropped it in.

"Forgot the hole," Mel said.

"Shit," I mumbled and in the end, I had to up-end the soup can over the container to fish everything out.

"I'll punch holes in them," Crowder said, leaving, and I started refilling the cans from the large bowl.

By the time I was finished, he'd come back in with four lids, all holes punched, all sides trimmed. Like before, I'd filled the soup cans to an inch from the top and put the lids on them. The number ten can, I filled to within two inches and then dropped the lid in. It wasn't quite trimmed enough, so I hammered it in with my fist slightly, being careful not to shred my hands on the sharp edges. It went in with little fuss after that.

"Sparklers in the holes?" Mel asked, and I nodded.

It was like when Maggie had brought home arts and crafts. I could remember one instance, where she'd had something that was made from straws and bows. Stick figures? It was like everything else in my memories. Fuzzy, foggy, and often it came out better in nightmares.

"What are the matches for?" Jamie asked.

I looked up. She had rejoined us, and she seemed more at ease than she had been the entire day.

"More of a timer than anything else. The sparklers will work to that effect, till they burn down to the thermite. We strike a match, wedge the book of matches over the edge of the sparkler, put the match in the other end. When the match burns down, it lights the book of matches, lighting the sparkler. I'm hoping if we can get in unseen, it will give us a good two minutes to set up the four thermite grenades and get out of there before the fireworks start."

"But they are fireworks," Mel said, in a sleepy voice.

"Pretty much," Steve told her, leaning over and hugging her.

100

THE DEVIL'S DUE

The green monster leaped to the forefront of my brain, and I had to fight it back. It was his family, not mine. God, what a mess I was in.

"So, we just wait for three am?" Courtney asked me.

"I want to get a few hours of sleep in before we go. If we leave here at 3:00am, we can hit the camp by 3:45am, just when the night shift is getting tired. You guys are sure that they don't park the armor inside?"

"Yeah, I'm sure. They can't. There's no room. It isn't a big camp," Crowder said. "Maybe twenty acres. Most of it is under roof for their electronics projects or for housing people."

"The components that they are forcing people to make?" I asked them.

I got nods all around.

"Lots of lights?" I asked, knowing some of this already from Courtney.

"Yeah," Steve said. "Most of them are on poles up high. The thing is, they burn out fast, running on those big diesel generators. I don't think they keep a proper voltage."

"Any of you good with a slingshot?" I asked.

I got blank looks all around.

"Anybody here have a slingshot?" I asked.

Mel raised her hand slowly, and I smiled. Everything was falling into place.

* * *

The alarm had interrupted a nightmare, but that

101

was par for the course. Courtney had fallen asleep in the chair, her feet up on the bed. I nudged her and she awoke with a start. I put a finger to my lips to make sure she didn't wake everyone, and after dressing, we slipped downstairs. Immediately, the smell of coffee assaulted my nostrils and I looked around. Everyone from earlier was sitting at the kitchen table, apparently waiting.

"Couldn't sleep," Steve said with a grin.

"So you couldn't wake us up to join the party?" I asked.

"No, you two are going to be going all ninja here soon. Figured you needed the rest. We've been monitoring the camp by radio. Still have a couple of people out there. The camp seems like the mobilization was a drill, or they've changed their minds. It's all confusing as hell, plus we're getting pieces of intel from Texas about the New Caliphate attacking an Air Force base."

"Hard to say," I said with a yawn, not knowing anything about the New Caliphate.

Beth walked out of the kitchen with two plates. Toast and eggs. Not a lot, but enough to whet my appetite.

"Thanks," Courtney said, taking her plate, "Any coffee left?"

"Yeah, I'd kill for some," I agreed, yawning.

"In the carafe, over there," she nodded to the table.

We ate quickly, and I took the wrist rocket that Mel had left on the table before she'd gone to bed. We suited up in new vests and grabbed the guns

THE DEVIL'S DUE

we'd been using, and we were ready to go.

"Have your scouts pull out slowly, and watch for any additional NATO forces or other movement," I told Steve.

"Already done."

"Ok, looks like we're about set. I'll see you folks in the morning," I said.

"Be careful," Jamie said, and Steve gave her a sharp look.

She noticed it and looked back at me.

"We will. I'll keep your deputies back, Steve. This mission is about sabotage and sapping their lines. No big firefights, if we can help it."

"What if something goes wrong and they give chase?" Steve asked.

"Then we spring the trap that we've been burying around the countryside," I said, smiling.

"You almost hope they follow you back, don't you?" Jamie asked.

"Depends on them. If we hit them hard enough, they can't do much without attacking us with civilian trucks."

"Yeah, that didn't go so well for them last time," Crowder said, chuckling.

"It didn't for us either," Steve reminded him, and the chuckling cut off immediately.

* * *

I didn't really need a driver, but the last thing I wanted to do was have to remember directions back to the farm. These men had been living and

103

working either at the camp or the farm long after the grid had gone down. In a pinch, they'd be two more guns, proficient to some degree. I knew Courtney was an OK shot, not as good as the deputies, but I trusted her. I knew she'd have my back, and she needed some payback. For the first time ever, I'd met someone who had worse nightmares than I did. Killing somebody wouldn't make mine go away, but for her, revenge might. Or it could make it worse. Still, she wanted this, and I needed somebody at my back that wouldn't run out on me.

"Nervous?" Courtney asked.

"Always," I admitted.

"I'm not, for some reason. I thought I would be, but it feels like just one more thing to do."

I pondered that. Maybe it was possible she'd already accepted her own death. I remembered reading about Samurais who adopted a mindset like that. It took away their hesitation. If they already considered themselves dead, they would be fearless and would be able to fight without flinching. Emotionless battle masters, ready to sacrifice themselves as needed to win. I hoped she wasn't thinking like that, but I could see how it might be useful. I'd been there at one point in my life, but that had been when I'd given up hope of ever seeing Mary and Maggie again. I wasn't the same man that I was a year ago.

"I'm not even going in and I'm scared shitless," Crowder said.

"That's cuz you probably shit your pants, by the smell of it," a female deputy said, punching him on

THE DEVIL'S DUE

the arm.

"Hey, easy on the gun arm, Frankie. I might need it later," he said in a falsetto voice.

Oh shit, this was the other woman. Frankie.

"Yeah, for pulling your head out of your ass," she told him in a stern voice, but I looked up to see that she was smiling.

We were in an old truck with a crew cab. We'd chosen it because it was the second most quiet vehicle the farm had on hand, and the quietest one was already out there, playing mobile scout, all blacked out, with the drivers wearing NVGs.

"Are we there yet?" I asked in the same falsetto voice, and everyone groaned.

"You just want to blow stuff up and shoot some bad guys," Courtney said quietly.

"Well, that sounds like a good way to start off the day. Besides the coffee. Can't go shoot bad guys and blow shit up without coffee."

"You're a trip," Frankie said. "Is it true, what Mel said about you?"

"I don't know what Mel said about me."

I knew who she was because of Steve, but I was probably the only one in the truck who knew that I knew. Courtney wouldn't have known, but most of Steve's men would. I hoped he told Jamie soon. Still, her coming along gave me a chance to look her over. She was in her late twenties or early thirties. Younger than Steve or I; probably closer in age to Courtney. I couldn't make out more than a blocky shape because she was wearing a vest, the same as the rest of us.

105

BOYD CRAVEN

"You're some kind of Spec Ops badass. You had to go underground in Chicago, literally, because you killed too many bad guys and they wanted to get even."

"Sounds about right so far," I told her, "but there were no cops around to stop the rapists and murders."

"So you did? The same way you did at the gate?"

"Pretty much. Except for a couple of times where I had to get creative."

"The trap house? It sounds like you like blowing shit up. I was on the detail digging out your Oklahoma City Bomber brew and burying the barrels."

"I learned demolitions a long time ago. Some from training, some from a couple of special forces dudes who were into specialty ops."

"Really? Like what?" Crowder asked.

"Well, there's this one guy who went by King. I don't even know if that's his first or last name. Just King. Big as a damned house and as mean as a rabid grizzly bear. He was a master of guerrilla warfare. Between him and a guy I worked with a long time ago named John, I learned a ton of dirty tricks to make things go boom."

"John…" Courtney said, "Isn't he the guy that…"

"Yeah," I told her.

"What's that?" Crowder asked.

"At the trout farm where y'all sprung me from, they thought I was John Norton. I know him, did some work and training with him, but I'm not him, and I haven't heard from him in fifteen years or more."

THE DEVIL'S DUE

"Why would they think that?" Frankie asked.

"No clue. Most of the folks I knew from the way back are dead. King, Sandra, Mike, James, Martin… John is the only one I know who's still alive. Retired. Last I heard, he was going to be a preacher or something in Alabama. His kid was growing up to be a missionary. Last I heard, he was."

"You stayed in touch?" Courtney asked me, surprised.

"No, but I hear things. The list of guys like us is a pretty small one."

"You were into uh… black ops?" Frankie asked.

"The blackest. I had a team that was in on for the hunt for Bin Laden, but we never found him. Lucky for him."

"Why's that?" Courtney asked me.

"Two of the men in my squad had family in the towers when 9/11 happened."

Everyone fell silent after that, until a few minutes later Frankie turned and asked, "So you *are* capable of doing what you're proposing to do? This isn't a suicide mission for you or us?"

Suicide mission. Should I read more into the question? Why had she volunteered to come? She knew that Jamie and Mel were back, she'd made herself scarce, and this was my first time meeting her.

"None of us have to die tonight," I told her. "It'll be lighting a few fuses, taking some potshots and running like hell. We just have to be careful to not hit any friendlies. Depending on the response, we might use the tow chain in the back and see how strong that fencing is."

"It's electrified," Crowder said.

"It won't be, if we do it right," I said with a grin. "Steve had some supplies, you folks liberated. I've got a pound of C4 and a few detonation pencils in my pack."

Courtney punched me in the shoulder lightly and I looked over. She was smiling, and for the first time since we'd been driving in the truck, she felt something. I could see it in her eyes.

"Getting nervous now?" I asked her.

"The anticipation is killing me."

"We're stopping in a quarter mile. Have to walk in from there," Frankie said. "We'll pull off and let you folks out. We'll keep an eye from afar."

"Good deal," I told her. "Courtney, ready to make things go boom?"

She smiled and held up a soup can, showing duct tape holding the lid down on the inside of the can, and turned it side to side. I had to smile at her antics. Maybe she could heal after all.

"I'm ready to watch their world burn."

Her words chilled me more than I liked to admit.

* * *

The problem I saw immediately, was that the light poles were positioned to cover the front of the camp in front of the gates, with guard towers at the corners. There were more than four vehicles there, too. That sent a shiver of worry through me. The

108

THE DEVIL'S DUE

NATO troops had joined the DHS in the time since we'd had our briefing at the dinner table not an hour earlier. There was an APC with a turret and an extra Hummer with a .50 cal. The vehicles with the turrets became my first priority.

Using hand signals, I led Courtney in a wide arc around the camp, careful not to kick any gravel and make unnecessary noise. There wasn't much cover in the open, so we stayed at the edges near the corn. If somebody was looking for intruders using night vision, I might get a chance to pull us into a row of corn before we were seen. If they were scouting for somebody using thermal, well… we were fucked. I didn't have anything for that, not in my handy dandy backpack. Not this time.

Reaching out and grabbing several rocks from the gravel, I found a few that were more or less squared off equally. A smooth round rock or ball bearings would have been ideal, but there hadn't been any ball bearings at the farm and the rocks here were from whoever had given the government the cheapest price. Still, it would work. I pulled the wrist rocket out, hoping that Mel had kept the band out of the sunlight, and put the rock in the leather pocket and did a test pull. It held. I looked at where the vehicles were that had the turrets and figured out a light pattern that would get us the best chances. Would the guards notice three lights going out?

I estimated that it was close to twenty yards from the front gate to the closest vehicle, and if I took out the lights to make an approach to the ones I wanted to take out…

BOYD CRAVEN

"What are the chances that they left the keys in any of these?" Courtney asked me.

"A lot of these just have an operating sequence to start them up. Mostly push button," I said, looking at some of the armor sitting here.

A lot of it was Russian surplus, stuff I knew all too well. Still, I had my eyes on a Hummer. It didn't have a mount, but what it had was an old M2 Browning .50 caliber machine gun. A nefarious plan started to form. I pulled back the band on the slingshot again and took aim. My first rock hit the shroud around the bulb. The rock punched a hole through the plastic and shattered the bulb, sending that portion of the lot into darkness. It was a lot louder than I'd expected.

"Is the generator surging again?" I heard someone yell.

I looked, it was somebody in the eastern tower who'd walked to the edge and shouted down.

"Probably," a man yelled back.

He wasn't inside the fence. I saw him walk up toward the gate. He must have been between two of the trucks, and in our arc around the lot in the darkness, we hadn't seen him. Maybe he'd been in one of the vehicles?

"Damn it. It's almost the end of our shift. Let the morning crew deal with it."

Music to my ears. I didn't pay attention to the shouted response, instead I focused on the next light and took aim. My rock missed it, and deep within the camp, I heard it hit a metal roof somewhere, making a racket as it fell. Without pausing,

110

THE DEVIL'S DUE

I loaded the slingshot with the last of my rocks and fired again. This time with the angle, I hit the bulb instead of the shroud and the light tinkled as the glass broke and the light winked out.

"Another one? Shit," the guard called. "You watch the gate, and I'll go get the scissor lift."

"Not like I'm going anywhere," the man in front of the gate replied.

I squinted in the darkness and I couldn't see into the western tower, but Steve had told me that nine out of ten times, that one was never staffed. It didn't have a heater or bathroom for long shifts. Still, if they had the NATO kids here to play, would it matter? Would it be staffed? From what I could see, it looked like they were gearing up for an assault and I could only guess where that assault would take place.

I turned and took the carbine off my shoulder and handed it to Courtney. She started to take hers off as well, but I stopped her and held a finger up to my lips, whispering, "I'm taking out the guy by the gate. Then you and I are going to set our charges, and take that Hummer with the M2."

"M2?" she asked, looking around.

"The machine gun."

"Oh, ok."

We'd have to ad-hoc our plan, as a lot of the hardware had rear-mounted engines. We could also put our ordinance on the turrets or barrels, disabling their big guns. That wouldn't be as ideal as disabling the engines on everything, but when I opened the show with the Ma Deuce, things would get interesting. Courtney would have her chance for revenge as the .50 cal BMG rounds chewed up the lightly armored vehicles remaining. Or at least that was the plan I had in my head.

"Be right back," I said, pulling my Kabar and holding it in my left hand.

I gave her one more look and saw she was melting into the shadows again, and I nodded. She'd come when I signaled her, I was positive. Slowly, I crept vehicle to vehicle, staying in the shadows as much as possible, my eyes everywhere. For the watch towers. For sleeping men in the vehicles, for the guard that I could no longer see. I had three rows of vehicles left to cover when I heard a soft whistling and then, the sound of a trickle of running water. I crouched low, being careful not to let the gravel crunch as I did so, and looked under the body of a troop carrier. A pair of boots stood on either side of a growing puddle.

Luck. More luck than I could have ever wished for. I ghosted around the front of the vehicle and chanced a look. A man in a black uniform with a DHS patch on his shoulder was urinating near the side gas tank, his carbine resting on the step of the truck. When I sunk the blade into the back of his neck, severing his spinal cord, he never made a sound. Just a quiet gasp as his life ended quickly. I pulled the knife out, wiped it off on his shirt and pushed his bloody corpse underneath the vehicle, then made my way back to the outer line of vehicles.

I saw the darkness move, and a blonde-headed specter stepped into the edge of the light and then back out of it. Courtney. She'd seen me coming back. I looked at the gate and the towers. Seeing nobody, I motioned for her to join me. The gravel crunched and I tried not to wince at her noisy approach, but there wasn't anybody within earshot. I thought. Hoped. We'd only seen one guard, and I'd put him down. I took my carbine back from her and slung it over my shoulder.

"Place these two on the hoods of that one, and that one over there," I told her. "I've got this one, that one with the big gun, and then we meet at the Hummer."

"We don't have enough of these," Courtney said, handing me the big can and a soup can full of thermite.

"Won't need any more, not if we're lucky. Even if we only take out these four, it's going to hurt their operations. Buy us some time."

"To blow shit up and kill bad guys?"

"Yeah," I said smiling, "to blow shit up and kill bad guys. Be careful, I only saw one guard roving outside the fence, but there might be drivers sleeping in some of these vehicles. If gunfire breaks out, just head to the Hummer that I pointed out."

"Got it," she said and started moving, this time a lot more quietly than she had been on her approach.

My heart was going a thousand beats a second by the feel of it, and I crept to my first objective. When I got there, I positioned the large can over where I knew the engine housing was. It was the most heavily armored vehicle, almost a full battle tank. I wasn't 100% sure if a couple pounds of thermite would do the job, because I knew a regular grenade was iffy… but it was my best chance. I didn't want this puppy coming our way. Still, I wasn't going for the main engine, so much as the controls to it.

The reason I hadn't filled the cans to the top was I wanted to create a wind break for the matchbooks. When the sparklers lit, it would throw off a lot of light and smoke, drawing attention. When the thermite went up, well… that was going to be huge light show, one that would blind you if you looked at it directly. I pulled out one of five matchbooks and pushed it into the can so the sparkler was behind the matches. I pulled one off, bent the flap backwards, and struck it. It lit and the quick smell of sulfur filled my nostrils as I shoved the lit match into the book.

I knew I had about thirty seconds roughly, until the main matches went up, igniting the sparkler, so I gave the area a quick look and almost sprinted to my second objective. It was an APC with a turret. I could get to the motor easily on this one, so I set my charge on top and placed the matchbook. I caught a whiff of sulfur and heard a hissing behind me from where Courtney was. One was lit. We had seconds now. I folded the flap back and started to strike a match.

"Hey, who the fuck are you?" I heard and I dropped the lit match into the can, hoping I'd done enough.

I didn't say anything, my body tensed as I turned

114

THE DEVIL'S DUE

and saw a man in all black and NVGs coming up on me, his carbine already aimed. Apparently, he hadn't gotten the memo that we didn't want Murphy to tag along for this op.

"The Avon Lady," Courtney whispered behind him.

The man was good, but she'd gotten into position before either of us had realized it. When she plunged her knife into the side of his throat, he almost dropped his gun and she ripped the knife out, severing his jugular and windpipe.

He started to fall, but in his last moment, he pulled the trigger, firing a three-round burst into the ground. Just that fast, I heard a hissing right behind me and I took off running, grabbing Courtney by the hand. She hadn't had time to wipe the knife off, but she sheathed it quickly, her hands covered in blood.

"It's starting," she told me as we made it to the Hummer, our hearts hammering so loud, I imagined all of the camp could hear it.

As it was, our running had masked the sounds of shouts all around us. We heard them, but couldn't make out the words. I shoved Courtney into the Hummer and went toward the back where the M2 .50cal was. Old Ma Deuce was ready to go by some kind soldier from somewhere. I pulled the charging handle and looked for targets.

"A stick shift? Is that why you brought me along?!" Courtney yelled at me, annoyed.

"Deal with it." I told her, looking to see how much time we had.

BOYD CRAVEN

When I opened this up, everyone in a mile would be awake.

"I want some revenge," she told me.

A bright flash of thermite igniting drew my attention, and with the extra light I could see a group of men running toward us, goggles on. They were still on the other side of the fence, but I wasn't going to let something like a little chain link and electricity keep me from doing my duty. They had no idea I was there, so I opened up. The M2 is a heavy machine gun, able to penetrate light armor, and was perfect for the mop up I had in mind. Still, it was a finicky beast. It was known for misfires, misfeeds, and it would cook off if you fired more than, say, 150 rounds in a couple of minutes. Depending on the ammunition, it could either be deadly or cause more harm to the gunner than those being gunned down.

As luck would have it, it was loaded with armor piercing rounds. Too bad the men running for the gate didn't know that. The quick bursts cut them down in seconds. I swiveled the gun and started putting short bursts into the front ends of the vehicles around me. All four vehicles with thermite were lit up, as the rust added the oxygen needed to make the exothermic reduction-oxidation reaction. Yeah, even a Devil Dog knows fancy words. Sue me.

I wasn't firing enough rounds to permanently disable vehicles, but enough to put them out for a day or two. Still, when I got the angle on it, I holed fuel tanks, causing pretty blossoms of flames. The

THE DEVIL'S DUE

Hummer rumbled to life and I was jostled out of the middle as Courtney pulled herself up and started firing at the fence line with her carbine. I was stuck reloading belts from some ammo cans and almost dropped the belt, but I held onto it. Courtney laughed and screamed and cried. Small arms fire started from one of the guard towers as I got the belt in and the charging handle pulled back. I swiveled, almost pushing Courtney out of the way with the now glowing hot barrel, and fired a short burst.

Wood splintered and somebody started screaming as the small arms fire stopped.

I turned and let loose on the west tower, then held my rounds and waited as Courtney changed mags.

"You having fun yet?" I asked her.

"No." She started firing again.

Inside the gate were highway concrete dividers; a chokepoint for people and vehicles coming into the camp. Cover for small arms fire. I waited until Courtney was changing mags to start firing at them where the men were positioned behind them. Chunks of concrete started disintegrating, and not wanting to be hit by flying concrete shrapnel, the men closest to my concentrated fire moved to reposition. Courtney took the opportunity.

"Got them."

"We've bloodied their noses enough. Get us out of here," I told her.

"Got it. You keep their heads down, Dick."

I wanted to pull the gates down and free everyone, but I hadn't seen the opportunity to do it yet,

117

and then I heard three motors rumble to life near the front of the gates.

"You were right about their drivers," Courtney yelled.

Rounds started pinging on the armor plate next to my head on the turret, and I dropped down.

"We're going to have company."

"We going to crash the gates?" She asked.

"Get us out of here. Get us to the…"

"Where are the damned lights?" she screamed.

"Go, just go dammit," I screamed as rounds started hitting the back of the truck, some punching holes in the light armor. I flattened myself out as we started moving.

The fire intensified for a moment, but once we hit the darkness outside of the lighted area, the pings of small arms fire came less frequently, until we were a good thousand yards away and it stopped entirely. Headlights lit up our back end and I popped up in the turret. I couldn't see what was following us, but I made sure the M2 was ready, turned it, and started firing at the lights. The barrel had had a good chance to cool down, so I let a long string of ammo go straight down the paved road behind me, hopefully disabling everything. What happened was the headlights went out; shot out or turned off, I'd never know.

"There they are," Courtney screamed.

For a heartbeat, I thought she meant the DHS/ NATO peeps, but as I turned the turret, I saw somebody waving with a flashlight in both hands. Frankie. Somehow, she'd seen me and recognized

118

me in the turret. My admiration for the young woman grew.

"Let's go," Courtney screamed out of the window.

Suddenly, a contrail of smoke and fire flashed past us, slamming into the truck. The explosion lit up the night as Crowder and Frankie's bodies were thrown, burning, into the air. I turned to see two men with a Javelin Anti-Tank missile launcher putting their sights on us as one of them reloaded.

"Get out of the Hummer," I said, crawling out of the top and rolling down the side till I hit the ground hard.

"What?" Courtney screamed out of the side window.

She was half out of the door when I'd made it to my feet, and I grabbed the front of her vest and yanked her unceremoniously out. The body of the Hummer and the angle of where we'd come to rest had shielded the movements, but now I couldn't see the missile men either. Despite the roaring flames of the truck, I pulled the screaming and kicking woman into the corn as a missile hit the Hummer. The shockwave of the explosion made my ears pop, and the heat wave was like standing next to a smelter.

"Thank… thank you, Dick," Courtney said when she realized what had happened.

We waited and another missile struck the Hummer, flipping it. We both ducked as debris peppered the area.

"Are the cops…" she said looking around.

BOYD CRAVEN

I could see Frankie. I crawled over to her, amazed by how far she'd been thrown. If being half burned hadn't killed her, the broken neck from landing did. Her body was shredded by shrapnel. I didn't see Crowder anywhere nearby.

"She's gone," I said quietly.

I motioned, remembering there were still men out there, and we started crawling deeper into the field. We were leaving easily followed tracks on the ground, but we were mostly covered overhead by the leaves of the corn stalks. You'd have to be almost ground level to see us. We heard motor sounds and shouts and screams of anger and rage.

Still, we kept going until I called a stop.

"That didn't go as good as I'd thought," I told Courtney, taking a drink from my canteen and handing it to her.

"I think that first missile was meant for us," Courtney said.

"It was. It passed us by a hairsbreadth."

"Luck."

"Not for Crowder and Frankie," I told her darkly.

"We all knew the risks going in. We're not out of it yet, Dick. Don't give up on me now."

Motor sounds coming up behind us somewhere on the road had us both ducking down.

"Stay? Go? Try to radio the farm?"

"It'll take them forty-five minutes to get to the farm. I figure, of the vehicles that left, most are probably headed there, but a few are behind, looking for us."

"Good, then I have more people I can—"

120

THE DEVIL'S DUE

"Make the call, and let's see what the morning sun shows us, if we make it that long."

Her teeth flashed bright white in the darkness.

CHAPTER 9

Throughout the night, we would sometimes hear what sounded like motor sounds rising and falling, gunfire, and sometimes either a large explosion going off or a large round firing from a turret. The wind had to be carrying just right, because we were far off. It wasn't long to wait on sunlight, though. It was close to six am, by the time we could see enough to make out smoke in the distance.

"Do you think they knew it was us, and that's why they went after the farm?"

"No," I said after a moment.

We'd been walking almost parallel with the road, sometimes venturing out of the corn to make sure we were still heading the right direction. Never before had I seen so much corn. I'd read about the

THE DEVIL'S DUE

endless waves of grain and corn in Stephen King's book 'The Stand', but I hadn't ever expected to be walking through a Nebraska cornfield, after an all too eerily familiar apocalypse. One caused by human fuckery, much like the super flu that had killed much of the earth's population in King's story.

"I think that if they *were* mobilizing to hit the farm, they were probably going to roll at first light anyway. They made it to the gate too fast. It was like they'd locked and loaded, and then got some shut-eye. I think they underestimated us as badly as we underestimated them."

"Do you think anyone's left alive? At the farm, I mean."

My feet tangled, and when I tripped, I didn't even try to stop my fall. My breath left me in a whooshing sound and I rolled to my side, dry heaving.

"Dick?" Courtney said, turning around in the narrow row and rushing to me.

It had been bothering me in the walk through the corn; was there anyone left alive? How would I deal with Jamie or heaven forbid, Mel dead? I pulled myself into a sitting position as my breath returned, and I wrapped my arms around my knees and put my face into them, to squeeze the memories and the tears away. Fighting off the flashbacks that I knew would be coming.

"Dick?" I heard cornstalks snapping and breaking, and then strong arms wrapped around me from behind.

I needed the comfort, I recognized that I needed it, and I hated myself as I sat back and let her hold me.

"I need them to be alive," I said, trying to keep it together. "I don't know if I could stand to bury Jamie and Mel."

I felt Courtney press her face into the crook of my neck, and she let out a sob herself. I took deep shuddering breaths and realized that she'd had to do just that herself, with her love, Luis. I was again a source of her pain. Feeling horrible, I was about to tell her so, when she spoke.

"I know what you mean. I don't want to see it either. We've all be through so much. All of us. If it happens, I'll be there with you. You won't go through it alone."

"Thanks," I said shakily and felt her remove her arms.

I put both hands on the ground and pushed myself to my feet. I made sure my carbine was clear of dirt and mud from my fall and stood straight.

"How far away are we still?" Courtney said after a moment.

"More than five miles. Probably closer to ten."

"How can you tell?"

"We would have run into the spot where we set up the ambush for the vehicles, starting at the five-mile mark. They weren't perfect, but I talked to Steve. After we left, he was going to have people manning them, in case there was a counter-strike."

"So, you two planned for everything?" she asked as we started walking.

"I think so, everything but what—"

124

THE DEVIL'S DUE

The rising sound of a motor made us both tense up.

"I have to—" Courtney started saying.

"I do, too. I have to know it's not them."

She nodded, and we started moving laterally until we were only one row in, then both of us got low and waited. Anybody driving through would be less likely to notice us close to the ground, than if our heads and shoulders were readily visible. Besides, it made for a smaller harder target to hit if we were seen. So we hunkered down and waited, neither of us speaking.

"I hear a radio," Courtney said, "like, country music."

I listened hard, and despite the grim situation, I smiled. I heard it, too. Hell, I even recognized the song.

"Cuz the girls are so pretty," Courtney sang to herself suddenly, breaking the silence and making a crow startle into flight from within the corn somewhere.

"Big and Rich?" I asked her.

"Yup," Courtney said, a smile tugging at the corner of her mouth.

The truck came into view, the rising heat from the asphalt making it a shimmering image I could barely make out, but what was unmistakable was the color of the truck.

"Is it?" I asked Courtney.

"I think so," she said, sounding hopeful.

We stood and waited as Steve's big truck rolled into view, half a dozen deputies standing in the bed of the truck, rifles bristling from every corner. Country music blasted from the old tape deck that Steve had stored in the EMP-proof bunker.

"Hey," Courtney called, stepping into the open and waving her arms.

I walked out behind her, trying not to smile too broadly. My face already hurt. Laugh, cry, it was amazing how quickly our emotions could take over our whole demeanor. We both waved our arms as the truck slowed and pulled up next to us. I squinted and frowned, seeing Mel sitting in the passenger seat, but was even more pissed to see who was driving.

"Steve," I said, walking up to the passenger door.

"Hey, Dick, you two, ok?" he asked, reaching his right arm out of the window.

"Yeah, barely. Hey Jamie, Mel," I said, seeing Jamie looking us over from the driver's seat.

"Is… where are the others?" Steve asked after a moment's hesitation.

"They had anti-tank missiles," Courtney answered for me.

Jamie and Mel winced, and the men in the back of the truck lowered their heads at hearing of the loss of people they had worked with, lived with. Steve choked up and silent tears fell from his eyes. I knew why, but I might have been the only one. Jamie looked at her husband, and in an instant, I realized that he hadn't told her. Hadn't had that talk yet. Like Courtney had tried to save me before, I was going to help this man.

"We've lost so many since the EMP," I said,

clasping his shoulder with my hand, "and it never gets easier losing men. Trust me, I know."

Hopefully, that would be enough. As he wiped at his face, he took a deep breath and looked at me, nodding. Message received, was what that look conveyed to me.

"What happened at the farm? Why are all of you out here?" I asked.

"They came for us, just like you said. We blew the first charge as a troop carrier went over. Dick, I think we used too much," Jamie answered. "Then, about a mile away, the secondary charge went up, flipping two of the trucks that had decided to keep going. Nobody… It was really hot. We thought if the wind changed directions the fire would spread to the farm, but…"

"Nobody was left," I finished for her.

They all nodded.

"The wind shifted and we've been firefighting for an hour now. That wasn't a fight, Dick, that was a massacre."

"I'm sorry," I told him. "Any of ours hurt?"

He shook his head no.

"Why were there so few vehicles?" Courtney asked me. "It sounded like over a dozen passed us as we left the area."

"I don't know. Maybe they turned off and headed south? But we didn't really get a good count of how many passed us. We were trying to hide out, more than anything else."

"We heard word of them bugging out, and you're right, Dick, they headed south. I was on the radio, monitoring everything, and folks I know on the horn reported a convoy heading that way, sixty miles away."

"So, what's that mean for the camp?" I asked, "We probably disabled everything we could there. How many guards do you figure are left?"

I asked Steve this, because he was looking off into the distance, and unless he wanted to tell his wife about his affair, he needed to keep things in focus. With Frankie dead, he may not ever need to burden her with knowing that her husband had thought her dead, and had replaced her spot in bed with a younger woman.

"Not that many, not according to the uniforms we saw in the carrier. It was probably half the contingent of the... and the other half..." he stumbled over his words.

"Ok. So, you guys are heading there to recon or are you...?" Courtney asked, letting the words trail off into a question that I had been wondering myself.

Why were they out here, and why were the men in the back silent and uncomfortable, and the ladies out of the safety of the farm?

"When you guys didn't come back, we found Mel trying to hotwire Dad's car," Jamie answered.

Mel shot her a withering glare. "Mom, they weren't home yet and it would take a NUKE to kill Dick. I knew they were stuck, and you two were busy."

"So, you decided to do your own rescue mission?" I asked her. "Do you even know how to
128

drive, kiddo?"

"This one's an automatic," she said proudly, and I had to smile at that.

A lot of post apocalypse cars and trucks were predominantly stick shifts for some reason.

"So, why did you let the women come?" I asked Steve sharply.

One of the deputies coughed while muttering something that suspiciously sounded like "asshole" and I looked at him sharply. He turned his head, his ears turning pink. The urge to beat his ass came and went quickly.

"With a bum leg, it was either ride bitch or let them go alone. Jamie pushed the kid out of the driver's side when she convinced her she'd drive, and the guys wouldn't let me leave without them."

"Rescue party. Search and Rescue," Mel said. "You wouldn't have left it to fate, not if it was us out there."

"No," I said after a long moment. "I wouldn't have left you two out there."

"Get in," Steve said, nodding to the back of the bed of the truck, "and we can go over it some more back at the farm. I'm just worried that later on they'll be coming back with more troops from somewhere."

That sounded credible, and I nodded.

"Thanks, guys," I said into the cab of the truck, and smacked the door panel as I headed back to the tailgate.

The back was pretty full, so I dropped the tailgate and hopped on it, letting my feet dangle.

Courtney joined me and together we put our rifles across our laps as Jamie executed a pretty good U'ie in the middle of the road and headed back.

"Do you think they'll be back later on?" Courtney asked me as the wind whipped around us.

"I don't think so. Not unless the vehicles that went south hook back around. I shot the shit out of everything at the front gate. The trucks that came must have been the farthest ones out, where I couldn't get the armor piercing rounds at an angle to shoot them."

* * *

We slowed where an enormous crater had taken out the middle of the road. The truck could only pass by going to the far corner and then riding on the median. To go any further, would have meant going through the corn, not something we ended up having to do, thanks to Jamie's fancy driving. It amazed me that the barrel of ANFO had created all that destruction, but what I didn't see was the troop carrier or APC or whatever it was they had had to use the demolitions on.

"Where is it?" Courtney asked me as I was trying to figure it out.

I stood, stepping back into the bed, and looked. In the corn, about twenty rows in was a smoking vehicle, most of the fire around it having burned itself out.

"Over there," I said pointing.

Courtney joined me and whistled softly.

THE DEVIL'S DUE

"Do you think you had them use enough?"

I let out a little chuckle and turned to her.

"No," I said smiling.

We hit a bump and somebody behind me grabbed onto the back of my shirt before I could stumble, and I thanked him and sat back down.

"Let's rest up and we'll talk about what comes next, after we get to the farmhouse."

"I just wish we would have come back with Frankie and Crowder," she said, flopping down next to me.

"Me too, kid. Me, too."

* * *

The men who were dispatched to do mop up duties on the DHS and NATO attackers were back early. There had been only one survivor and not much in the way of salvageable materials. More than once, people complained about using too much ANFO, but in a joking manner. They knew that if every vehicle had rolled that had been planning to, the farm would have been overrun, without the tricks and traps that had been set in advance.

After a day's rest, three quarters of the men left at the farm went to the FEMA camp to scout how many guards were there. There was a lot of radio chatter and the name Offutt Air Force Base came up a lot, especially on the scrambled channels that the DHS and the NATO troops had been using. Steve wanted to recover the bodies of Frankie and Crowder, and I'd told him where to find Frankie in relation to the wreckage.

But we never got a chance to go in person. Radio intercepts suggested a ton of movement, and we were only mentioned once in relation to the troop movements. That had me stumped, so I decided to go check things out and listen in, live, instead of through the hourly briefings that Steve had shared earlier. There was only one problem: the long range radio equipment was in the bunker, with the antenna running from the barn's roof to a telephone pole, so cleverly hidden that the only way it would have been found out, was if a lineman had come out to service the now non-working electrical service.

"Why do you look so green, Dick?" Courtney asked me, "You'd think you'd be ok with going underground."

I nodded and got up from where I had been resting. Getting older, it seemed like I did more resting than not, but then again, how many guys my age were still running, gunning and getting shot up, dinged and beaten on a regular basis? Sure, I was a little apprehensive about going down into the bunker, but for a lot of different reasons, and none of them had to do with my own fears.

"Let's go, just watch our backs down there. We've still got a lot of people that are pissed with us, and Scott's wife and kids are down there."

"Is he the dude that Doc shot?"

I nodded. Scott had been a hothead, an oxygen thief of the worst sort, but I doubted he'd been evil. He was a father, and probably in his little warped mind, had thought that shooting me had been the right thing to do, but he'd paid for his belief with his life. Now, I was walking into the lion's den, where I may or may not run into an angry mob. Still, getting the intel about the DHS and NATO forces secondhand wasn't cutting it. Besides, I could get on the horn and maybe do a little poking of my own. It was getting later on in the day, and I knew I should hurry, or Beth would have our hides for missing supper.

"Just keep an eye on things. I'm going to play with the radio."

"I didn't think you knew how to use them?"

"I know the basics. I mean, I'm not going to kick Steve's radio guys out. I'm sure he's got two operators down there monitoring things most of the time. It's what we would have done."

"He was pretty smart for getting into HAM radio stuff, then? I always thought those people..." she let the words trail off and turned sort of red in the face.

"Were dorky?" I asked her, chuckling as she nodded. "Come on. Let's go see this bunker."

We left the house, and for the first time, walked to the barn together. I'd never been inside, and although Courtney had, in the time since we'd been back, she hadn't been inside the bunker. She knew where it was though, so I followed her. Turned out the barn looked a lot like any old barn on the inside. Wooden rails separated what looked like horse stalls, and a couple had horses in them, something I'd missed seeing around the property while I had been recovering. The smell of manure was a little

133

overpowering in the closed up barn, but as we approached, one of the horses whinnied and pushed its nose over the partition I was walking past.

I felt its warm breath on my shoulder and neck and turned, taking half a step back. I almost stumbled, but Courtney grabbed me by the shoulders and steadied me.

"He's just getting a whiff of you. You never been around horses?"

"Not this close," I admitted, "Camels, yes, horses…"

"You're a good one, aren't you?" Courtney said, reaching down into a galvanized metal trashcan that had been set just outside of the stall and pulled up a handful of dark, sweet smelling grain.

I almost pulled her hand back when she offered it up to the horse, but it gently took the grain off her hand, licking it. I was a little dumbfounded, and wondered what sort of history this woman had where she had such an affinity for large animals.

That was when she wiped her hand on my shirt and laughed, darting to the end of the rows and inside the last stall. Seemingly, she disappeared. I followed, looking at the goo on my shoulder and when I got to the stall, I smiled, forgetting her prank. There was a long trapdoor propped up and a staircase leading down. I looked at the door a moment and saw that the side that would face up when closed was covered with a rough, muddy colored carpet. It was cut to fit in such a way that the wood wouldn't flex if you were to step on it, but I doubted a horse could walk on it without going through.

THE DEVIL'S DUE

Still…

"Come on," a voice said from the depths of the staircase.

I went down, curious. The staircase was made out of concrete and what looked like polished fiberglass walls with two ninety degree turns. In all, I guessed we were twenty to thirty feet underground by the time I'd made it to the bottom. I stopped and admired what looked like a semicircular stainless steel blast door that was open a couple of feet, with Courtney hanging onto the inside of it.

"This place is cool," she said, the excitement evident in her voice.

I nodded and followed her in. On the back side, the door had hydraulics in place to quickly assist in the opening or closing of the door, and that was a bit of a surprise. The door was thick, but I hadn't thought it was 100% metal, but evidentially it was, or damned heavy. The walkway in front of us was circular, or more semi-circle. If a twenty feet diameter tube had been cut in half, that's what the rest of the hallway looked like, but more of the polished fiberglass look with lightbulbs in wire cages every ten feet along the ceiling. It was about thirty feet long, and at the far end, it opened up, but I couldn't make it out because of the brightness of the area.

"Look, this is their… storehouse?" I asked, motioning to the steel racks that lined both sides of the walkway.

They were stuffed full of boxes of clothing, spare blankets and pillows, and case upon case of freeze-dried food. A further ten feet down, was almost an entire floor to ceiling shelf, full of home-canned foods. Then another shelf had medical supplies… I turned and the opposite side of the hall was just as diverse in supplies as anything else.

"I've never seen so much food…" Courtney said slowly, letting her fingers trail across boxes of supplies as she walked toward the opening.

I gave up my own gawking and went to the end of the hallway, and looked. It opened up into a circular room that was at least fifty feet in diameter. Other hallways, like the one we'd left, went out in eleven other directions. After a moment, I realized that this was like a central hub and the hallways were the spokes. It was like being inside a great big wheel. I took a few steps forward, turned around and looked again. The number '12' was painted above the opening. I turned and one through eleven were painted in a clockwise manner. This didn't look like any government bunkers I'd ever seen, and I supposed it had to have been a commercial or custom bunker.

The cost of this had to have been astronomical, and all the supplies… I was spinning around, trying to take it all in when Courtney nudged me and pointed. Near three o'clock, were several couches set up in a U shape and kids, ranging from early teens to young adulthood, were jumping up and down and shouting at each other. I couldn't quite make it out, but I heard about free parking, so I surmised it was a heated game of Monopoly. I couldn't help but smile.

The ceiling didn't have the bulbs in cages like

136

THE DEVIL'S DUE

the hall we'd left. It was recessed lighting and the walls and ceilings were the same high gloss white fiberglass material. It actually made the room a lot brighter than I thought it would. A kitchen and long bar with stools on both sides took up another section. The last third of a section had tables, chairs, and on one old wooden bench, what looked like radio gear with two men sitting in front of it.

"What are you doing down here?" A young voice startled me, and I spun.

For half a second, I thought it was Maggie, but I caught myself before I could turn it into a bad situation.

"Hey Mel, we came down here to check out the radio. What are you doing?" I asked her.

She turned a little red, the biggest giveaway was her ears. They were almost purple with the flush.

"Is it that Billy Stevens I heard the girls talking about?" Courtney asked her, giving the kiddo a bump with her hip.

"No!" she said a little too sharply, drawing glances from the half a dozen people walking by.

I grinned. "So, if it isn't Billy, who is he?"

"Oh. My. God. Stop, please?" She was so serious, and for half a second, I thought she was going to spell it out. O. M. G.

"Ok, which one is he, though?" I asked her, "So, I'll know who to shoot first."

"Dick… not cool, man," Courtney said.

I smiled and watched as Mel slunk off and headed down to a tunnel marked with a three. I half expected her to flip me off, and then remembered that Mel wouldn't do that. I'd just expected that sort of reaction to the teasing I'd given her.

"What? You were that age once. You gotta know what it's like," I reminded Courtney, not wanting to be the last one ribbed, like I always was.

"Yeah, hormones, acne, no self-confidence… great time to be a kid… Besides, what were you like at sixteen?"

"I was…" I let the words trail off.

I thought about it. I remembered an old Camaro, I remembered working as a bagger at an old Hamady's store in… and it was gone, just like a lot of my memories. They faded into the mental fog that had made my life difficult, sometimes making me forget who was who, and sometimes forget where I was at. I used to be worse, but over time, things had been getting a little better. Maybe, part of it was getting closer to the end of our journey.

"I think I was pretty normal. A walking hormone."

"Oh God, I think all boys are at that age. There's the radio."

I wanted to call her Captain Obvious, but she knew I had already seen it. I started walking and just figured it was her way of changing the subject, or diverting attention. As I passed the tunnel marked '3', I could just make out sleeping cots on one side, three high, stacked end to end as far as I could see. Mel was leaning against a shelf on the other side, talking to somebody and laughing. Maybe this would be the new normal? Finding happiness wherever we could.

THE DEVIL'S DUE

I was almost knocked off my feet as a woman plowed into me. Her nails flashed, and I felt pain on the side of my face. For a brief moment, I thought she'd gotten my eye, but she must have missed it as I'd jerked my head away from her instinctively. Spittle flew from her lips as she screamed, but I didn't hear anything. I grabbed the hand that had raked my face, and grabbed the other wrist when she started slugging me.

I held tight, but pushed her away from me when she started trying to bite and head-butt me. As soon as she got some distance, her foot flashed out, catching me between the legs. The pain was immediate and I felt nauseous. I fought the urge to fall to my knees, since I had her wrists pinned. Instead, I turned my hips so she couldn't get another shot in, and started squeezing her wrists tightly, trying to get through to her.

"Lady, stop," I kept saying over and over.

Behind her, Courtney walked up and took her pistol out of her holster. I wanted to scream at her to stop, not to shoot her, but she turned the gun so she was holding it by the barrel and swung it, using the butt to smash the woman in the back of the head. She went limp and I let her go, letting her fall hard on the concrete. All at once, the sounds of the bunker hit me. It was like I had a mute button and it had been pressed, then all at once, somebody had turned the sound back on with the volume pegged at max.

"Dick, are you ok?" Courtney asked, pulling for something in her pocket.

139

"Yeah, crazy bitch got me in the nuts," I said, watching as she pulled a bandana out of her pocket.

That was when I felt something hot and wet dripping down the left side of my face. I rubbed my hand through it and looked. Blood. I folded the bandana into a wad and applied to the wound to slow the bleeding.

A girl who was almost a teenager launched herself at Courtney, screaming, "Why'd you hit my mommy? Who are you? Somebody help!"

I was able to snake a hand out really quick, going for her shoulder or her shirt, but caught the back of her ponytail instead. Her momentum was too much and it was like a rug had been pulled out from under her and she shrieked. I let go of the ponytail as quickly as I'd grabbed it, and Courtney had already jumped to the side, the butt of her pistol raised, ready to strike at the new threat.

"The fuck's the matter with you people?" Courtney screamed as a ring of people started forming around us.

"You're the ones," a boy said, one of the Monopoly players.

"The ones who shot her dad!" Another pointed to the girl on the ground who was crying.

"You're the one who shot my Uncle Clay," a little girl said from between the bodies of the older teenagers.

"Oh shit," I mumbled to Courtney, "This is Scott's family."

"That's my dad, you asshats!" the girl on the floor shrieked.

THE DEVIL'S DUE

"Kid, get out of here," I growled. "Go get the doc for your mom. She just got KO'd."

"I wish you were dead," she spat, scrambling to her feet and taking off down the tunnel we'd exited.

"The fuck is going on here?" a deeper voice intoned.

I turned to see one of the deputies, half in uniform, approaching, his hand on his gun.

"Woman attacked me," I said, pointing.

"So, you knocked her out, attacked her daughter?" he asked, anger in his voice.

"No, I got kicked in the nuts, trying *not* to hurt her."

"Turn around, put your hands behind your back," he commanded, reaching for a pouch.

"That isn't going to happen. And if you don't get your hand off your gun, things are going to get real ugly, real fucking fast."

"Dick…" Courtney hissed, and I looked around.

Several people had handguns out, pointing down at the ground. Not deputies, but civilians. Down here in a concrete bunker, the shots would likely ricochet until they'd spent all of their energy. Not a safe thing.

"I came down here to use the radio. I didn't ask for this," I said, pointing to the woman who was starting to stir, a lump forming on her head.

"I said turn around, put your hands behind your back—"

He'd gotten within a few feet of me, and I let instinct take over as he pulled his gun from his holster. I flowed forward with a grace that was more muscle memory and practice than any conscious effort. I pushed his wrist down, gripping it hard with my left hand as I brought the knuckles of my right into his Adam's Apple. I tried to pull the chop to his windpipe so I didn't kill him, but it was a last minute effort as my reason kicked in before I let my training take over. He gagged and I looped my now free arm under his armpit, still holding his gun hand with my other, and used my hip to toss him over my shoulder. Did I mention we were near the wall of the tunnel? Just past number 3? We were, and when he hit it head first and slumped, I wasn't surprised. Courtney had seen me move and instinctively hit the ground, her hand over her head as I pulled the gun from the unconscious cop's hands and aimed it at the stunned onlookers.

"Anybody else want to play? Drop your guns!" I shouted, the revolver aimed at them.

"Just like you said before, you executed the refugees?" a woman asked from the back of the semicircle of people that had formed.

"Refugees?" I asked, "I didn't execute any..."

"The men at the fence, the reason why my husband was killed," the woman screamed, obviously the mother of one of the kids who had accosted me earlier.

"They were NATO and FEMA plants, not refugees. Now, I'm not kidding, drop the fucking guns!"

This time, I heard the metallic clanks of several pistols hitting the floor. I couldn't see everyone's hands, but my point had been made. I checked the deputy's pulse, and as I looked up to see what was going on, I could see Mel holding back an older boy who was red-faced with rage. She looked like she was holding her own, so finding a strong pulse, I pulled the cuffs from the deputy's leather pouch and dragged him over to the woman and handcuffed him to her. If I'd had two sets, I'd have put them back to back and cuffed them, but I didn't, so I couldn't. It was only a matter of time. Courtney had raised her pistol to cover me as I cuffed the assholes. Somewhere in the tussle, I'd dropped the handkerchief I'd been using to stop the bleeding, and I walked over, picking it up off the polished floor.

A red smear stayed behind and I debated just letting the blood drip onto the floor, but this was Steve and Jamie's place and it seemed wrong somehow. That's when I heard the distinctive sound of a pump action shotgun. Having carried one for many years, I recognized it and wasn't surprised when a new voice boomed out.

"You two, slowly put the guns down and put your hands up."

Again, the ricocheting rounds would be deadly down here and none of us would be safe, so I turned to see a familiar deputy with a KSG held up, not four feet behind Courtney's surprised face. I dropped the pistol and raised my hands slowly. Courtney was already following directions, having seen me doing the same. She looked me in the eyes, silently asking me for direction, so I shook my head. For now, we'd go along with this. If the fool opened up down here, women and children would

143

be hurt as well, something a cop should realize.

"Now, does somebody want to explain to me, what the hell is going on?"

Courtney moved to my side and we stood shoulder to shoulder, our hands raised chest high. Still, neither of us said anything.

"No? What kind of clusterfuck did I just walk into?" he asked, looking at the two stirring forms, handcuffed together on the ground.

"We were coming down to use the radio. I guess we weren't expecting to get attacked like this," Courtney said after a long pause.

"Attacked? They killed our own people, and now they've—"

"Rory, put down the shotgun."

I'd know that voice anywhere. I turned my head slowly to see Jamie striding toward us, her face a blank mask. If anything, I'd have to say there was more than a hint of anger in her eyes, but other than that, she was totally unreadable.

"Stay out of this, ma'am," Rory, the deputy with the shotgun said. "This is a law enforcement issue."

"This has never been a law enforcement issue," I snarled, surprising Courtney and half of the bystanders with the anger and conviction in my voice. "If you all keep looking at things like that, you're all going to—"

"What, die?" Mel asked, coming up and standing beside her mother.

I just nodded. Those two women hadn't been insulated from the rest of the world in bum-fuck Nebraska with a bunker to hide in. Those ladies had gotten out of Michigan with me, survived Chicago, and all the crazy bullshit that was my life. Hell, they'd been with me for a good chunk of time, and I didn't need to say anything more, because it would have been a waste. I was letting my crazy show again.

"Rory, last chance, put down the shotgun," Jamie said.

"Jamie, this doesn't concern you. Let me handle this."

"Rory, it does concern me, as well as your wife and kids."

The words chilled the air, and for a second, his eyes left mine and flickered to her.

"Anybody else who attacks these two while on my husband's property will be kicked out. I don't care that you've worked with him forever, or that you used to go bowling on the weekends… or even if you've invested in the bunker. You attack them again, I'll put you and your entire family out myself, or I'll die trying. Then, you can deal with Steve."

The shotgun's bore was huge, and I was staring right down it. I could see the deputy had it sighted in on my big, fat head. Still, his eyes flickered again and then he lowered it to his side. I took a deep breath and Courtney let out a huge sigh. She must have been holding her breath the entire time, and she wasn't the only one. Several people were looking around, their mouths hanging open comically like a fish.

"I'm just trying to assess the situation, ma'am," the deputy told her, his arms going limp as he let the shotgun drop to the end of the drop sling.

"The situation is, that I've been hearing a lot of misinformation from the people living down here. Dick and Courtney did not attack and murder our people. It was Doc who shot Scott, after Scott shot Dick in the back. When Clay was about to gun down Doc, Courtney shot him. The attacks you all are talking about came from the residents of the farm first. They were just defending themselves from us. As soon as I heard that Dick had come down here, I knew there would be problems. Evidently, Steve didn't fill you all in like I'd asked?!"

"Why should we believe him when it's our husbands who are dying?" somebody's wife shouted.

"Nobody is begging you to stay, if you don't like it here," Mel spoke up, and I felt a surge of pride for what she was trying to do. "In fact, this is really kind of our home, lady, so why don't you shut the—"

"That's enough, Mel," I said curtly, before the young lady got herself into some trouble.

I knew she was protective of me, she had proven it countless times. Rory shifted, and my attention once again focused on the KSG he was holding. I looked at it and started walking toward him. He made as if to bring it back up, but I kept my arms at my sides. It had all the same scratches, and when the cop saw that I wasn't going to attack, he looked at me, puzzled.

"Hello there, old friend," I said smiling.

"You're a nut job," Rory said. "And you have no business threatening to put out my family." The last

146

was said to Jamie.

"Dick, what were you guys coming down here for?" Jamie asked, her eyes never leaving Rory or the others.

I tried to swallow the frog in my throat, and in the half a heartbeat pause, Mel spoke up.

"They were coming down to use the radio. I headed down about the same time they did. They were teasing me about… well, they were teasing me. They need better information. Right, Dick?"

I nodded. "I knew I wasn't the most popular guy here, but I had no idea this shit show was going to happen," I told Jamie, "and I certainly wasn't trying to get arrested by these two assholes."

"You just hate cops, all cops," one of the teenagers who hadn't left the semicircle said.

"No, I was once a cop of sorts myself," I told him. "But like I said before, this isn't a police action. I just came down here to get more info. To help you folks out. Like I've been doing since—"

"Since the doc used up a lot of medicine getting you off drugs? Stuff we could have used to survive longer?" another voice chimed in.

It was a thin woman, holding a young boy and a girl on each hip. Twins, if I had to guess. They were towheaded and looked at us sleepily, the little boy holding a thumb in his mouth.

"Rory," Jamie said in a low growl I'd never heard before. "Get your woman under control. We don't need any more fighting like this."

"Infighting? Those two have hurt and killed our own and you're worried about *us* hurting *them*?"

147

BOYD CRAVEN

She screeched at Jamie.

"Melissa, calm down," Rory said, holding up a placating hand. Interesting, another Melissa.

"Why should I? Ever since Jamie got home, things have changed and everything's gone to hell. These two have done nothing but cause trouble, and you're sticking up for them? No wonder Steve wrote you off as dead."

"Excuse me?" Jamie said, her tone icy cold.

"Stop it, Melissa," her husband warned, louder this time.

"Steve's out there trying to get his girlfriend's body back and you're in here safe and sound, defending this scuzz ball. Whose side are you on? Maybe you're sleeping with him, too?"

I turned and looked at Mel and Jamie as the words sank in. Something inside of her broke and Mel looked at me, confusion on her face. I knew it wasn't about the half question/half accusation, but rather the bit about her father. I looked down and to the side and walked close to Rory, my head near his as I leaned in to whisper.

"I'm out of here soon anyway, but if your wife doesn't shut the fuck up, you all might be as well. She didn't know about Frankie. Steve was going to talk to her about it."

"Understood," he said through clenched teeth.

"By the way…"

"Yeah?" he said, meeting my eyes.

"That's my shotgun. You must have gotten it from the camp."

He hesitated half a second, and then took it off

148

THE DEVIL'S DUE

and handed it over to me.

"What's she talking about, Dick?" Jamie asked.

"Courtney, let's get out of here. I'll see if we can borrow a handset from someone," I told her, ignoring Jamie.

"Somebody want to tell me what's going on?" Mel asked, a waver in her voice.

A boy of about the same age stood next to her. I saw that he'd snaked his hand into hers and she was squeezing it back absently.

"No, not really," I said. "I think it's time for me to go home."

"Dick!" Jamie said in half command, half plea.

I kept walking. As much as I loved her, that was one set of news that wasn't going to come from me. I couldn't be the one to tell her, not without shattering her and leaving us both vulnerable. I was too raw, and leaving her would be the next hardest thing I'd ever done. I didn't want her last memory of me to be my telling her that her husband had fallen in love with another woman.

CHAPTER
10

I took the supplies I needed out of the front room and tried to ignore the screams and cries from upstairs. Steve had arrived home with the men, and he was already in a foul mood. Rory's wife's words must have stuck with Jamie because I kept hearing Frankie's name. It sounded like Steve was coming clean, something that couldn't have been easy. He'd been put in an almost impossible situation and now, he had to figure out how to go forward from here. I was doing the same thing.

"I don't feel right, taking this stuff," Courtney said.

We were both near the front door, getting stuff together. "Don't," I told her. "A lot of it came from the DHS and the FEMA camp."

"Oh, well…"

THE DEVIL'S DUE

"Dick?" Jamie called.

I hadn't noticed it, but the yelling had stopped and she'd made her way downstairs.

"Hey," I said, tying a sleeping pad on the pack.

"How long did you know?"

"So you know now?" I asked her, nodding toward Steve, who was just coming down the stairs.

"I told her," Steve said, his face set in a grim expression.

"Yes, dammit. It's bad enough my husband… but you knew, and you never told me?"

"It wasn't my place," I told her. "I knew the day before she died. Steve was trying to find the words to tell you himself… and once she was gone… I mean, that wasn't my place."

She opened and closed her mouth several times to respond but instead nodded, and then looked at my bags. "So, that's it? You're leaving?"

"I think our time here is up," I told her. "Trouble seems to follow me. More than that, though, it's time for me to get going to Mary and Maggie."

I didn't know what else to say.

"Were you even going to say goodbye?" A tear trickled down her cheek.

"Of course we were," Courtney said, reminding me that she was still there next to me. "We were just going to get a jumpstart on packing."

I shot her a thankful look. To be honest, goodbyes were not my strong suit, and I'd been thinking of slinking off while they were still fighting.

"I'm not leaving just yet," I said, trying to shoot her a smile.

151

"Good, because it would crush Mel and…"

"Hey, we're still here, aren't we?" I said, and she looked up and met my gaze.

I had to smile. She looked half ready to wage war on the world, and I didn't blame her. Her world had been turned upside down, sideways and then served with a bitter pill to swallow it down with. Still, my goofy visage probably helped break the tension.

"Dick," Steve said, walking up and putting a protective arm around her shoulders, "would you both stay through dinner? It's almost ready and I can make sure it's just Mel, Jamie, and I with you and Courtney."

I nodded, still smiling.

"I'm dying to know what happened at the camp," Courtney said, changing the subject, something she was good at.

"That's what I want to discuss with him. That and the Air Force Base."

* * *

If we hadn't been stopped in the bunker, we would have walked into what was happening around the country and the President's next address. Apparently, a lot had been going on in the world, and the DHS/NATO troops may not have been trying to attack the farm directly, rather, only retaliated when Steve's men and women blew the hell out of them. By the sound of it, they were bugging out to Offutt Air Force Base. Holding civilians had been…

THE DEVIL'S DUE

"Hey, listen to this," Steve broke in, turning up the handheld radio he always had on, and pulled the earwig plug out of the side and turned up the volume.

A voice, recognizable as the 44th President of the United States came over, strong and clear.

"My fellow Americans. Today, we've suffered the grave loss of Laughlin Air Force Base. Forces of the new Caliphate, supported by members of ISIL and North Korea, over-ran one of our southernmost military bases. At this time, all personnel are presumed lost or captured. A small force of American commandos and heroes tried to intervene, but they were also overrun and killed to a man.

"I cannot strongly enough renew a call for unity and request that all able bodied Americans check in with any military recruitment center, base or National Guard unit. Our Navy and Marines have still been tied up in land and sea operations defending both coasts, and making strategic strikes against our enemies in their homelands."

I looked at the others at the table in shock. Attacked at home... And losing?! They all looked as bewildered as me.

"Our country has undergone tremendous hardships, yet there are more still to come. Within our own government, certain departments have been working against our own country in a coup attempt. At this point in time, I am disbanding the DHS by Executive Order and by my authority during Martial Law. Those who served the DHS lawfully, may turn themselves in to be processed and their guilt deter-

mined. Let me say this clearly… From this moment forward, if you are approached by someone who says they are from the DHS, know that they are not a part of the United States of America's Government. Protect yourselves within the rules of law we have enacted.

"Furthermore, NATO resources are in the process of falling back to local Air Force bases to be evacuated. To say their presence here in America has been a disaster, would be an understatement. Most of the forces are good and trustworthy, but as with politics, there's been far too much corruption and I'm calling for every NATO force, not directly under American command, to return to base and be bivouacked."

"I'll be dipped in shit…" Steve muttered. "They were falling back?"

"Shhhh," Jamie said, and I shot her a grin of appreciation. Eat that, Steve.

"Now for the good news," the President said, and then coughed to clear his throat. *"Our camps in Kentucky have become models for America going forward. People are willingly working together, training together, and building the components we need to jump start the electrical grid in many parts of the country. The program that FEMA Director Jackson has come up with has become a model that has been copied throughout surrounding areas.*

"Kentucky, Alabama, Missouri and Mississippi have all been converted to Blake Jackson's new method, and everyone who wants to eat and work, can. Farmers are harvesting late summer and early fall crops, and with some good old American inge-

154

nuity, we've got dozens of old diesel trains repaired and working. Commerce and the movement of goods shall be starting, albeit a bit slowly.

"Power has been restored to parts of the Pacific Northwest, where we have refineries making fuel again, to power the plants needed to energize the Silicon Valley, to continue to speed the process.

"If you aren't working on rebuilding America, please consider helping defend it. When I have more to report, I will. Until then, God bless."

"That Muslim-loving, no good, piece of monkey feces. I don't believe him one bit," Steve spat.

"He did say that the DHS is now defunct," Courtney said, grinning slightly.

I nodded to her in return. It meant 'open season' on those bastards, and I knew Courtney was thinking the same thing.

"He's blaming everybody but himself. He hasn't ever even met with his DIA Chief of Staff, how does he even know the DHS is corrupt? He doesn't listen in to his own security briefings—"

"Steve, it's their last night. Please. Dick and Courtney were accosted here on our property, in the bunker. I'd like them to at least, get the information they were almost shot for."

"Listen, most of those guys would have done the same. It's training, second nature," Steve said.

"And Mr. Dick's second nature is to kill men who point guns in his face, yet he didn't," Mel told her father pointedly. "And he's really good at it, so obviously it could have been a lot worse for your officers."

Point for the squirt.

"I… Listen, what happened down there was unfortunate, and the way you manhandled my men, again, was unacceptable. I can't have that happen, so your decision to leave couldn't have come at a better time."

The entire conversation happened without Courtney and I opening our mouths to defend ourselves, yet I was ready to. The jealous green monster was rearing its ugly head again and I wanted him to trip himself up. As it was, he sort of did it himself.

"A better time? I heard you talk to him, the day you carried him upstairs," Jamie spat. "You wanted him gone from the day you met him."

Steve's resolve cracked. "You don't know that I saw the way he looked at you two? It was like you were *his* family! What was I supposed to have thought?"

"I don't know. Did you consult your girlfriend first?"

The words came out of Mel's mouth and Jamie let out a surprised sound, more of a shriek cut off on the opening note. A pregnant silence filled the room, and then Courtney started giggling for no reason I could tell. I looked at her in surprise, and she covered her mouth and shook her head at me. No matter what she was trying, it wasn't working.

"This isn't funny, dammit!" Steve shouted, his voice raising.

Jamie started smiling and then giggling herself, albeit more quietly. "Yes, it is. You're just an asshole sometimes. I love you anyway."

THE DEVIL'S DUE

Mel looked at her mom in surprise, and then I smiled at the look she made. It was like the girl had been asked to swallow a live squid or something equally disgusting.

"I get it," I said. "You don't like me. I don't blame you. For what it's worth, you have a wonderful family, and as you and your men have said… I'm a broken man. I'm not trying to steal them from you, and I understand you wanting to protect them, even from me. What I don't get, is how you can keep sticking your head up your ass. Instead of thumping your chests here at the farm, why aren't you all out there in the public, keeping the peace?"

My words quieted everyone, including the two cackling hens.

"We were, before," Steve said.

"At the camps. It looks like the camps have now been disbanded. As the highest elected official in the county, what the hell are you going to do about things now?"

Steve's face screwed up in deep thought. He started to answer once or twice, and I wanted to jump on the table, do an Irish Jig and say, "Your damned job, like you should have been doing all along!", but I didn't. Instead, I sat there and watched him suffer.

"You have the men, you have the comms, and now you don't have DHS and NATO breathing down your neck, unless they are renegades. And those are going to get hunted down, if the radio transmission is any indication."

He just looked at me, then turned and walked

157

toward the dining room table. With nothing else to do, we followed him.

"This is going to be the last time we see Jamie and Mel, isn't it?" Courtney asked me quietly as we neared the seats.

"Yeah. Hey, what caught your funny bone back there?" I asked her, wondering what had caused her outburst of giggles at such a tense moment.

"I wasn't expecting an open pissing contest between you and Steve. The look on Mel's face when she realized what was going on was priceless. Jamie…"

"Yeah, she must have seen it too, huh?"

"Yeah. It was priceless."

"Hurry up you two, I'm hungry," Mel said loudly.

Caught whispering, we joined them at the table to catch up and say our final goodbyes while sharing a meal.

CHAPTER 11

Leaving them was the hardest thing I'd ever endured, including when Mary and Maggie had left me in Chicago, all those years ago. It was a long teary goodbye that lasted half into the night. We were going to leave at dawn, taking one of the Hummers. Steve's men were working hard to make sure the DHS markings on the door were covered up, so we wouldn't be shot on sight because of the President's address, but we were basically taking the lightly armored version without a turret. Enough to stop casual potshots, but a pig on fuel. Luckily, it was diesel and there would be plenty of broken down semis on the sides of the road, and diesel lasts forever.

"This sucks," Courtney said for the fourth or fifth time, during my *first* hour of driving.

159

I didn't answer her. I was too raw, and I absolutely hated goodbyes. We'd said ours late the night before, and had gone to bed. This morning, we'd left before any of them had come down. If we hadn't snuck out, I wasn't sure I could have left, if I'd had to face the girls in person again.

"Yeah," was all I told her in response.

We sat there in silence. Steve's neighbor lady had baked us a couple loaves of bread, and we had fresh food in the form of bread and smoked sliced ham that would last us a day or two, and then two five gallon buckets of rice, beans, lentils and mixed veggies. Both of us still had our packs and we had enough ammunition for our guns to make walking uncomfortable. Still, there was a lot of empty space in the Hummer, even with the fuel cans in the back.

"Tell me about Mary's parents' farm," Courtney asked, after minutes of me weaving in and out of traffic.

"I don't know if it was the drugs, or what I've been through, but I can only remember flashes and snatches of it. We weren't there often. I don't think her dad liked me."

"Really? Somebody didn't like you? Who could believe that?"

I smiled at her sarcasm. In fact, it was a welcome change from the sullen silence of the morning.

"Yeah, the thing is, I don't know if it was any one thing, or the fact that she was his only daughter..."

"Dads are funny about daughters," she said, and then looked out the side window so I couldn't see her face. "Is it a big place?"

160

THE DEVIL'S DUE

"From what I can remember, it's forty or sixty acres sitting in the bottom of a valley between some hills. I remember one time, heading there with my buddy, Mary, and Maggs… It had gotten cold. People on those hills in Arkansas don't get much practice driving on the ice. If you don't have four-wheel-drive, you'd have a hard time getting there in the best of weather. When it was icy…."

I held up my hand and made the iffy gesture.

"Are there a lot of folks around the farm?"

"Just the old man, his wife, and Mary and Maggs. No neighbors, none that live nearby that is. It's funny, because it's probably the best spot in the entire state to hunt and fish. The stream that runs through the east side of the property is full of fish."

"So, I know I'm playing twenty questions and all, but one more. What's Mary like?"

I looked at her, and her gaze met mine. I started to tell her, but a flare flying up over the horizon drew my attention and I slowed the Humvee. Only forty miles from Jamie's farm, I saw. Shit.

"What is it?" Courtney asked, seeing it.

"Signal flare. Somebody's letting other folks know we're coming."

"DHS or NATO?" Courtney asked, a hint of eagerness in her voice.

"Easy, killer, I doubt it. They'd probably be using the radios they have, and they sure wouldn't have given themselves away like that.

"Then who the hell is sending up a flare?"

"There's no way of knowing," I said out loud, and slowed to a stop.

BOYD CRAVEN

I got my binoculars out of my bag and started looking around. It was corn almost as far as I could see, but off in the distance I could see telltale signs of civilization, as a small streamer of smoke drifted up into the sky to the left of the highway. I couldn't tell if it was from a campfire or a burning city, and we were still too far away to even smell it, but it would've been easy to miss if we weren't looking for it.

"Want me to get me to get the maps out and see where the nearest detour is?" Courtney asked me, getting her carbine ready from where she'd rested it against the door.

"Yeah, that would be a good idea–"

Another flare lit the sky from the same general direction as the first, but I started to get a sense of what was going on, and I didn't think it had anything to do with us.

"Dick? It looks like there's… There's more smoke coming from where that second flare landed."

That had been exactly what had caught my attention. They weren't using the signal flares to signal at all. Someone was setting fire to something, probably the near dry corn. It'd been a dry summer, and there hadn't been any rain since I'd gotten to Nebraska. Unless it had happened when I was unconscious, and that was always possible, but no one had ever commented on it. I shut the Hummer off and opened the door, pulling my KSG out with me, just in case.

We were a good distance away from whatever was going on, but it never hurt to be safe.

THE DEVIL'S DUE

"Dick, what you think…" Courtney started to say, but I waved her off with a hand and strained to listen.

The wind shifted, blowing the warm air back at my face, drying the sweat that had been building up on my forehead and hairline. What it also brought was the fragrance of smoke, and what sounded like two gunshots.

"Did you hear that?" I said to Courtney, across the hood of the Hummer.

"Yeah, gunfire. You think they're trying to burn someone out?"

"Something's going on. Let's get the maps out and see if there's any way around this mess."

Courtney went back to her seat in the Hummer and started digging through her pack, pulling out the laminated map of Nebraska that Steve had given us. It showed in great detail where the Air Force Base was and where NATO and the DHS were falling back toward, so we could avoid it altogether.

"What mile marker are we at?"

I told her, and I walked around the hood of the Hummer, the engine making a slow ticking noise as it cooled. Using her finger to trace the route on the map, I could see we were pretty much in the middle of nowhere.

"I think we'd have to backtrack a good hour or more and then try some of the service roads, but that would put us right back at Steve's farm."

"Well, there is another route," I said smiling. "We could make our own."

"You mean, just driving straight through the

163

corn, do a little Baja, some 4x4 action?"

Her smile was infectious, and I gave her a grin back. As much as I got involved in other people's business, I would like to be able to avoid a fight for once. The phrase came to my mind, and I don't even know where I'd heard it, "not my monkeys, not my mess". Unless something rather heinous was going on here, I was going to try to find an old two track, running through one of these fields. I knew the Hummer would be tough and rugged, but finding a spot to squeeze in without going over the guard rail would be interesting. I got back in and slammed the door shut.

"Probably something just like that," I said.

But in the back of my mind, I wondered if I really could pull this off and detour before being dragged into the mess.

"Go slow for a while, I'll look for something—"

That something didn't happen fast enough. Before I could start the engine, I heard the far off hum of motors, and they were heading our way.

"Get ready," I said, firing up the engine.

I didn't have a lot of choices, other than to turn around and try to hide the Hummer amongst the stalled traffic, but with cornfields stretching as far as I could see, there weren't many places to go. My best hope was pulling onto the far right of the breakdown lane, where a semi-truck had stalled and been abandoned.

"Can't we go over the guard rails?" Courtney asked me, buckling in.

"No, these were made to try to slow semis whose

drivers fall asleep. Speaking of which, I'm going to try to wedge us in," I said, creeping up on the semi. "Over there…"

The truck was half into the breakdown lane, stopped where it had rolled into another car that had died when the EMP had gone off. There was a tangled mess of metal and glass, but pulling up behind it, I thought if it wasn't too tight we could probably fit.

"Going to scrape the paint if you get any closer to the guardrail."

I knew that, but hearing her say it made me wonder if this was really a good choice or not. The Hummer we were in, even without the DHS signs painted on it, stuck out like a sore thumb. Out here in the land of Lincoln, it looked like everyone drove Chevy and Ford trucks, with small Japanese compacts being the norm for cars. This stretch seemed to have a lot more trucks, though. I hoped the driver of the car that the semi hit had made it out ok, but I doubted it, judging by the mess. Slowly, with a slight sound of metal on metal, I got most of the Hummer behind and beside the semi.

With any luck, they would keep rolling north, and miss seeing us in their rearview mirror.

"It's a truck," Courtney told me, looking forward while I worked on not tearing off my mirrors.

"Ok, I've got eyes on it, too," I said. "When they get close, make sure you aren't silhouetted. Duck if you need to."

"Yup," she said, scooting lower in the seat.

I did the same, just enough so I could keep my

head above the dash and watch the truck coming. It swerved side to side, in both the north and south bound lanes. The driving was erratic, as if the person behind the wheel was drunk. It was painful to watch, and as bad as the driving was, I started to relax, hoping that they were so intoxicated that they would pass us right by without noticing… until the truck tried jumping the median again, clipping a stalled car with its bumper. The back end kicked out, and instead of steering into the slide, the driver panicked and hit the tail lights as the rear end spun to face us.

"Oh no…" was all Courtney had time to say as the truck rolled.

I watched in horror as it rolled twice and slid to a stop, its mangled sheet metal coming to a stop, the truck resting on the cab.

"Come on!" Courtney screamed, and she tried getting the door open on her side.

"We're up against the guardrail, stop hammering the door!"

"It wasn't an adult driving!" she screamed.

"Oh shit," I put the vehicle in reverse.

This time, I left sparks as I hurried the Hummer in reverse till I cleared the back of the semi. I punched the gas, shooting the heavy vehicle forward. I hadn't even stopped when Courtney was jumping out of the door. I pulled the parking brake and followed, my eyes scanning the distance to see what the truck had been running from.

"Dick, he's alive, hurry. I don't know what to do, DICK!"

166

THE DEVIL'S DUE

I ran for the truck and crouched down to where the driver's side window was shattered out. A boy hung there limply, blood dripping off his head from some scalp wounds. Thankfully, he wasn't a big kid, maybe seven or eight, and when the truck had come to rest on the cab, he hadn't been crushed. Still, he was unconscious and still belted in. Knowing there were no hospitals, ambulances or right way to do things in an imperfect world, I tossed my KSG to Courtney and laid down on my back, scooting my upper body into the window opening until my head and arms were inside.

I could see the rise and fall of the boy's chest; it was shallow but there. I tried to avoid the blood dripping into my eyes, but it was almost impossible. I had to push his arms out of the way, but after a few tries and a lot of stress, I was able to push the button on his seat belt with one hand, and cushion his fall onto me as much as I could.

"Dick, I've got your legs," Courtney told me as I felt her hands wrap around my ankles, "You ready for me to pull?"

This was going to hurt.

"Yeah," I said and was surprised when I started sliding out.

My plate carrier scraped against the safety glass, crumpled metal and then the concrete, as the small woman pulled close to three hundred pounds of limp weight backwards and I tried to keep the kid from any more head or neck injuries.

"Oh shit, you're cut," she said, kneeling down.

"It's not mine," I told her.

167

She stopped and looked, and then knelt down, one hand going into her pocket. She pulled out a clean handkerchief. I took it gratefully and turned, starting wiping the blood off the boy's face. What it showed was I'd probably guessed too old, when I'd thought he was seven. I marveled that he could even reach the pedals, especially having been buckled in.

"Mom..." his voice was thick and phlegmy, and he started talking before his eyes even opened.

They fluttered and he opened them as I was wiping the blood out of the way.

"Get the first aid kit," I said, but Courtney already had it in her hands and was ripping packages of stuff open.

"Hey kid, you're going to be all right. Just relax a second and let me check you out."

"I want my mom," he said, his eyes welling up with tears.

"I'll fix you up and we'll go find her," I told him, taking an alcohol wipe and gently wiping at the cut over his left eye, the worst of the bleeders.

"Are you like a policeman?" he asked after a moment.

"I used to be something like that," I told him. "Other than the cuts, anything else hurt?"

"My head," he said, coughing and rolling to the side.

He vomited, and I held him on his side so he wouldn't choke. I'd seen his pupils; one was wildly dilated, whereas the other wasn't. Concussion. When he was done, I gave him the handkerchief, the clean side, and watched as he spat and then wiped his mouth and chin before dropping it on the pavement next to him.

"Let me see you move your other arm, then your legs and toes."

We went through the whole process, and while I was cleaning him up, Courtney was as white as a sheet. She kept grabbing more and more supplies, using butterfly bandages on all of the cuts. Some of them could have probably used a bandage, but I wasn't going to stop her. I was near panicked myself. Where had he come from, and why was he driving a truck?

"What's your name, buddy?" I asked him.

"Ricky," he said, pulling both hands to cover his eyes.

He moaned and rolled to the side again and dry heaved. There hadn't been much in his stomach to start with, by the look of it. Still, as he retched, I noticed he wasn't overly thin from hunger, nor did he have the telltale signs of scurvy, something I'd run across overseas when people only had one choice of food and not enough fruits.

"I'm Courtney," she told him, breaking the silence. "Where's your momma and papa?"

The words sounded funny coming out of her mouth, but he rolled onto his back again and stared at her for a long moment, focusing on her face.

"Back at the farm. They shot my daddy and Momma told me to run. I tried to get my sister to come, but she hid in the barn. I took the farm truck, Daddy always said I could use it at the farm, but

I was so scared, I jumped in and… they shot my daddy." He broke down in tears.

Half of me wanted to go to pieces and break in half, the other wanted to fly into a mindless rage. I didn't know anything though, didn't know anything.

"I think he's got a concussion," Courtney told me.

For a moment I was angry, I wanted to scream that it was obvious, but then I realized that it was like every other battle I'd been in. Anger let the reason seep out of me, until I questioned my own actions after the firefight was over. I needed information, and I needed a plan.

"Let me talk to him really quick, Dick," Courtney said, pulling out some more alcohol wipes and handing them to me. "Clean yourself up a bit."

"These are my damned monkeys now," I growled.

"What? Dick, you're… Seriously, clean up. I need to see if you got tore up when I dragged you out. I'll talk to Ricky."

I didn't know why she was talking to me like that until I saw her eyes shift from me, to the boy, and back to me. I looked down, and my fists were clenched so tight that blood was welling out of one hand where my nails had broken the skin of my left palm. I unclenched them and took the handful of wipes. I shot the kid a look and saw he was still scared, and probably scared of me. I walked back toward the Hummer, taking the KSG off the ground where Courtney had left it. I wanted the map.

CHAPTER 12

I felt like I had been walking for hours, but in reality, it was probably five minutes or less. The farm was about two miles up the road. It didn't have a driveway off the highway, rather, there was a gate across their fencing so that large farm equipment could be moved between fields. The boy had crashed the truck through the gate and had made his journey north to where we'd found him. His dad (Robert) had been in the barn with Ricky, working on a John Deere, when they'd heard the rumble of a truck's engine.

They'd had so few visitors at the farm since the EMP, and they had hoped it was their cousins coming to see them. His little sister, Rebecca, had been playing in the dirt with some of Ricky's old matchbox cars, in the drive between the house and barn when a strange-looking truck with the back loaded with men had pulled up. Robert had told his daughter to get in the barn and hide when he saw that everyone holding a rifle. Ricky remembered that his dad had put his pistol down on the workbench, so when the shooting had started, he had been the first to fall.

"Run, Ricky, get your sister and run," their mother had called from somewhere near the house.

Ricky had run toward the barn, where his sister was hiding. He'd remembered to grab the keys to the farm truck off the big nail his dad kept them on. It was an old thing, no good for road driving because it had a bad "tied rod and busted hubs", according to the kid. He'd tried to convince his sister to come out of hiding, but she hadn't. Men had burst into the barn, running from the hay storage on one end, to the stalls, screaming and shouting. One had fired at Ricky and he'd ducked, starting the truck and shifting it into drive.

"I didn't want to leave Becky," he said over and over, crying in Courtney's arms.

"How many?" I asked Courtney.

She probably told me already, but I couldn't hear very well with the blood pounding in my ears.

"He says, he thinks six or seven," she said without looking up.

"How old is Becky?" I asked.

"She's four," he said, a cough almost turning into a gag. When he got it under control, "I'm six though, so I'm the oldest. Miss Courtney, can you and your dad help me?"

172

THE DEVIL'S DUE

That got me in more ways than one. Of course I was going to help him, but I wasn't going to correct him about Courtney. I didn't have time. I'd seen what assholes did to women and children, when there was nobody coming to arrest them. I thought I'd left most of that behind in the flames of Chicago. Apparently I was wrong, and it was time to find his family and see if any were left alive.

"We can't move him right away, Dick. His concussion… and someone needs to stay with him…"

I pulled her gear out of the Hummer and started stacking it on the side the guardrail was on. It would have to be enough… but I couldn't leave them in the middle of the road. Or could I? I dug into my pack and found the old camo netting. It would stand out some if people were up close, but with the corn and weeds on either side of the highway… from a distance it might just blend in. Courtney saw what I had and nodded.

"I'll need your canteen," she told me, and I gave it to her without asking what or why.

"I left you one of the handheld radios. I'll check in on channel three. Steve said all these were programmed the same. Give me two or three hours before my first check in. I'm going to creep up close and walk in."

"Just like before," Courtney said, nodding at me.

"I just pray there's nobody with anti-tank missiles this time."

"Probably some rednecks." She stood and then walked over to me, kissing me on the cheek. "Be careful, *dad*."

173

BOYD CRAVEN

I gave her a slight shove at that and she snickered, before returning to where the gear and kid were. I unrolled the netting and threw one side over her, letting her shade the kid. He'd propped himself off the hot asphalt and onto some of the packs, so I was hopeful that the concussion wouldn't have long lasting effects. If he could move himself a few feet… Shit, I wasn't a doctor, but I knew a little more than most people when it came to first aid.

Such as how to perform an emergency tracheotomy, coupled with how to slit throats silently.

"I'll be safe, kiddo," I said to Courtney and the snickers stopped.

* * *

I almost missed the gate. I'd expected it to be much closer to the farm, but when I saw it off its hinges, I backed up and pulled the Hummer into the tall grass, and then pushed a new hole into the corn where I turned it off. I hoped the hot exhaust wouldn't start a fire, but anybody who tried to track the kid would find the Hummer. I was hoping to be in the middle of the field, so hiding it shouldn't have been necessary, but old habits die hard.

I considered my plan. I had no plan. I pulled my pack close and grabbed the extra dump pouch and clipped it onto my vest. My KSG had a loadout of 00 buckshot and slugs. I reloaded it with all slugs, putting buckshot in one pouch, the slugs in another. I left my bag and started moving out slowly. Daytime operations were not what I wanted to play

174

THE DEVIL'S DUE

in, but I hadn't set the chess pieces up here. Ricky said his father had been shot, but had he actually died? Played dead? So much I didn't know.

In the distance, I could make out the roof of either a house or barn over the stalks of corn, but I couldn't tell. Ten sweating minutes later, I could make out that it was a barn and I slowed even further to look, listen and smell. I definitely smelled something smoldering, but I couldn't tell what it was. It wasn't wood smoke, and it didn't have the plastic death smell that burning houses did. I pondered that and left the trail, walking through the rows of corn, using the metal roof in the distance to keep me on the right track.

Corn silk and chaff covered me, and I could feel what felt like a thousand paper cuts as I pushed through into a new row, giving me a view of the farmhouse. The barn was on the other side of the house, but its bright red roof was what I'd been seeing. The house looked intact and I walked between the rows, surveying the opening in the corn that they'd given themselves for a lawn. A homebuilt sandbox was full of plastic buckets, shovels and Tonka trucks. An older, yet not quite rusty swing set hung, with a baby seat replacing the center swing. I hoped that had been for one of the two kids.

They both had R names. My mind drifted while my body and senses kept working, looking and making sure I was clear as I circled. R names. Robert, Ricky, Rebecca and their mother had an R name, but it sat at the tip of my tongue. I couldn't quite…

BOYD CRAVEN

"Shit," I heard, the voice carried to me on a soft wind.

The barn. The large side door was open, and although the two story house and dark windows hadn't been cleared yet, it was the barn I was focused on. I started moving quietly, pushing my way through to get a better view. One truck sat in the gravel driveway, a man leaned against the passenger side front tire, a bloody hand held over his chest. He wasn't moving and I couldn't see his chest rising and falling. Probably dead.

I didn't know who the truck belonged to, and should have asked Ricky what their everyday truck was, because it would let me know if this was theirs, or the raiders' or...

"Shit, shit, shit. Why is this taken apart?" A male voice screamed from the open doorway and then the sound of something heavy hitting the concrete made a ringing sound, like a tuning fork that had been hit.

"Can you fix it, put it back together?"

I was thirty feet from the barn now, and I left the corn, moving in a slow crouch toward the corner of the building.

"Yeah, but it's going to take some time. I wish I knew what he was working on."

"What do you mean?"

"You fucking shot him! He could've been doing a tune up, or was pulling the block to change a bad piston out. We won't know now. All I can do is put it together."

"If it doesn't fire up, we'll tow it back with the

176

THE DEVIL'S DUE

truck."

I heard some grumbling reply, but couldn't make out the words.

"Good thing about that basement pantry, though. Never knew these guys were preppers."

That perked my attention up some and it made sense why there weren't six or seven voices. They had probably loaded up one truck, and left these two behind to get the tractor. Probably tow a trailer with it back to whatever hole they'd crawled out of.

"They took them," a voice said behind me, startling me.

I spun and aimed at the man who I'd thought was dead.

"My wife and daughter…" a bubble of blood formed at his lips and burst, covering his lips like a bad lipstick job before his head slumped and his hand fell away.

"I thought you said that asshole was dead?" the second voice shouted.

A man wearing bibs and a sweat-stained white t-shirt strode out with a large pistol in his hand. He started firing into the corpse of Robert without even looking. I waited, knowing he hadn't seen me crouched nearby. I had a bead on him, but didn't want to get ambushed by more men. I still didn't know how many had been left behind. I didn't have long to wait though when, seeing no reaction, the hick turned just as I pulled the trigger. The shotgun roared and his head evaporated from the nose up in a gory Rorschach of blood and brains against the side of the barn.

BOYD CRAVEN

"Frank?" a man asked, his voice full of fear.

The man I'd shot had fallen, most of his body out of the doorway. His work boots and part of his legs would be visible to somebody inside. I pumped the shotgun and waited.

"Oh shit," whoever it was said again.

"You really need to work on your vocabulary," I said as I rolled in the doorway.

The man was in his late sixties, his hair a greasy gray mess that was barely contained by an old Donald Trump red cap. "Make America Great Again," it exclaimed. In his right hand was a rag, and the left had a large wrench. I didn't see any guns, but that didn't mean he didn't have any nearby. My eyes darted around to the barn and I couldn't see anybody else. I already had the shotgun pointed at the man, but I raised it to point at his mouth. He dropped the wrench.

"Who else is here?" I asked him.

"Nobody, did you... Frank's my cousin, you didn't need to do no killin'," he blabbed.

With the rag, he started wiping at his hands, wringing them together.

"Like you killed Robert?" I asked, moving closer.

"That was Frank, he said that Robert went for his pistol, so he got the first shot off."

I looked at the workbench, where Ricky had said his dad had left his gun. It was there. The old man's gaze followed mine and when he saw the gun, he looked back at me, his pallor going even whiter than it had been before.

178

THE DEVIL'S DUE

"Who else is here?" I asked him, butting the end of the barrel under his chin and standing to my full height, making him back up half a step and get on his toes as he pressed himself into the wall of the barn.

"Nobody, I swear. We were just coming to talk to him about some food, then the shooting started."

"I didn't ask you what happened, asshole. Where's the woman, the little girl?"

His eyes darted to the left. "I don't know, they weren't here."

I wanted to pull the trigger, decorate this side of the barn as well, but instead I held the shotgun in my right hand and reached up, pulling my K-bar free from its sheath on my chest rig. I held it up, showing him the black finish, and the glint of the sharpened edge. I slid to his stomach and pushed until the man was trembling, though I hadn't even broken the skin.

"This blade is big enough to go through that fat gut of yours and into your kidney. I can promise you'll die from it, but it'll hurt badly first. If you don't tell me where the woman and kid are, that's how you're going to die. Screaming in agony."

His skin had started going grey and he turned to the side, coughing. I knew I was pushing him, pushing hard, and he was liable to have a heart attack or a stroke at any second, if he didn't break.

"Ben took 'em back to his place. Him 'n' his wife lost a kid. With all this food, they'd be set and I promise, he ain't' gonna hurt that kid none."

"What about the mother?"

179

His eyes shifted to the left again, but he didn't answer. The lie almost left his lips.

"Why didn't you take that truck?" I said, putting the knife back in the sheath and taking half a step back.

"My cousin was gonna drive it back, when I got the tractor up and running."

"One last question," I said and paused as the old man clutched his chest over his left side, staring to dry heave.

I waited until he caught his breath. "Where do I find Ben?"

"That's my son," he said, coughing.

Tears of agony or real fear filled his eyes, and he shook his head at me. I got that, no matter what, he wasn't going to betray his son, if he thought I was going to kill him.

"I'm just here to get the mom and daughter back to the son. I'm not going to do any more killing. This isn't my squabble, if y'all aren't planning to kill the kids."

The man looked at me, looked at my vest, the pouches hanging off it. The pistol and knife were close by for easy access. When he moved, it would have been comical, if it hadn't been so tragic. He reached for my pistol as if in slow motion. I stepped back and kicked him in the sack. He fell to the ground, almost hitting the edge of the workbench. He moaned and rolled onto his back. His right hand massaged his chest some more.

"Where do I find Ben?" I asked him.

He told me, and I wasn't surprised to hear that

they lived close.

"You promised, no more killin', I want to hear you promise again."

"Sorry, Pops, I lied."

He gasped from my betrayal and from the pain he was feeling.

"It's my heart, my nitro…" He looked at the workbench.

A few feet away, just out of reach, was a prescription bottle. I took it and looked at it, before pocketing it in a dump pouch.

"My heart, I've got a bad ticker."

The shotgun roared, and he fell silent.

"Yes. Yes, you did."

Walking out, I dug through Frank's pockets for the keys. I didn't have any particular qualms about looting the dead, but the whole inbred Deliverance-style fucking family was getting to me. Father, son, cousins… all in on the robbery, murder and kidnapping? I'd seen it before and I'd probably seen worse, but at that moment, the pounding in my ears was louder than the sound of my own raspy breath.

They were expecting Randy with the pickup, so I pulled Robert's corpse into the shade of the barn; I'd rather have covered him up with something, but nothing came to mind quickly. I hadn't seen tarps, plastic or any canvas close by. Every second that the mother and daughter were with Ben, the potential for danger would keep mounting. I fired up the truck, marveling that of all the dead vehicles in the world, this farm had two working trucks, even if one of them was a jalopy.

BOYD CRAVEN

This one was in pretty good shape, an old Dodge with a diesel motor. It fired up without issue and I hit the gas pedal, watching a black plume of smoke come out the back. Putting it into gear, I left the way the old man had told me. I spared a look back to see if I could see where the flares had landed, but I couldn't see anything close by. Must have missed whatever they were aiming at and it was in a corn row somewhere.

I didn't have time to hunt for more trouble, so I focused on the small country road I'd pulled out on. Two miles down, I would make a right onto main street, and it was the third driveway on the right. That sounded easy, but when I turned onto main street, I found the first driveway easy enough. The second driveway wasn't more than half a mile away. Had the old man lied to me? I felt in my pouch for the pill bottle, remembering there was an address there. I started pulling it out, but a green sign and mailbox came into my view. The numbers matched. I slowed to a stop.

I knew the sound of the motor would travel, but I wanted to go in slow. The driveway was faced with two old tractor tire rims, the old steel ones, and the mailbox sat next to one, leaning on it drunkenly. There was an old Ford in the driveway, backed up to what looked like a pole barn. It was by far, the newest and nicest structure on the property. The house appeared to be an old trailer, sitting on cinder blocks. A figure came out of the pole barn and waved. I couldn't make out what he said with my window down, but I thought he shouted 'come on

182

up'.

I drove up quickly, the truck bouncing me back and forth as I navigated the rutted driveway. The figure turned his back on me and started walking back into the barn with a box of something. I slid to a stop and put it in park, leaving the engine running. Again, adrenaline flooded my veins and I felt damn near invincible with the rage and tunnel vision, but I had to fight against that. I had to save the woman and girl child. It's what my Mary and Maggie would want me to do. Those who can help, should. That was my Mary's favorite saying.

"Hey Randy, give me a hand with—"

He walked out of the barn just as I sank the blade into the base of his skull. He was younger, mid-thirties, if I had to guess. Not any more though, he'd never have another birthday. The scent of vacated bowels filled the air and I let him drop where he was without moving the body. I'd heard screaming and crying from within the trailer. I moved from the barn to the truck, using it as cover, and then approached the trailer. I didn't have to get on my toes too much to look inside a dirty living room window. A woman was tied to a kitchen chair with cotton rope. She was sobbing and calling to a little girl, who was curled up on her feet.

"You need to quit this and tell the girl to give me her name!" A second woman screamed, and I saw the bound woman's head rock back from a slap.

The one doing the slapping was about the same age as the dead man, thin with hunger, with tangled brown hair.

183

BOYD CRAVEN

"She's my daughter, you can't just take her from me," the bound woman sobbed.

In a low voice that I probably wouldn't have been able to hear if the windows hadn't been cracked, the brunette growled, "I've seen the way Ben looks at you in church. I always hated him and you for that, you know? But maybe, I'll give you to Ben as a play toy and you can have more kids for me. Would you like that?"

My blood ran cold. I moved to the porch. It was a wooden and fiberglass ordeal, with the railing falling off on one side. I peeked in and saw that the shrill woman had a knife in one hand, and the screaming and pleas were so loud that I couldn't stand it anymore. One heavy boot shattered the cheap screen door, tearing it from the jamb. Before it hit the ground, the KSG fired. The shrill woman was thrown backwards, and I rushed in. The little girl was curled up around Mary's legs, and my wife screamed as I pulled the K-bar from its sheath. She quieted when I cut her wrists and handed her the knife.

"Maggie, it's ok, baby girl," I said, scooping my daughter up.

If anything, she just bunched up into more of a ball, screaming for her mother.

"Put her down, asshole," Mary growled.

"It's ok, Maggs, it's fine, I took out the bad guys."

Something hard punched me in the back, and I spun and heard something clank to the ground. It was the K-bar. She'd stabbed me in the trauma plate. My Mary had...

184

THE DEVIL'S DUE

"I'm sorry," I said, handing the shocked woman her daughter, and recovering the knife. "Heat of the moment confusion."

"Get away from me!" she cried, looking at me and then the fallen woman.

"I'm not with them, I'm here to help you," I said. "Your son got away and crashed. He's not hurt bad, but he needs you."

Her face calmed when I spoke of her son and she did a double take when I mentioned the crash.

"Is he ok?"

"Yes, he's got a concussion, but his first words were for you two and Robert."

She looked down at her daughter, who was quieting, and I could see a couple of green eyes poking out of a mass of blonde hair. I didn't know how I could have mistaken her for Maggie, but I'd done it again and…

"Who's Maggie?" the little girl asked.

I sighed and looked to the woman's corpse, praying the little girl hadn't seen that, and looked her in the eyes as much as I could.

"I was worked up when I came in here. For a minute, I thought you were Maggie, my daughter."

The little blonde head nodded once and she turned in her mom's arms and buried her face against her.

"My husband?" she asked, her words trailing off.

I shook my head. She bit her lip and nodded, fighting back the emotions. She'd had to have seen, but not known for sure. I'd thought he was gone

185

BOYD CRAVEN

when I'd first seen him. A dilemma suddenly became apparent in my mind.

"Do you know who the rest of the men were?" I asked, knowing how small towns could be.

She nodded, tears running down her cheeks.

"Do you know how to drive a stick?"

She shook her head. It wasn't impossible and it would mean doing some backtracking, but it was all possible. With her husband dead and one kid hurt, the other traumatized, I wasn't going to just walk away. Not yet. When I decided to get involved, I made it my problem and I wasn't about to walk away from it.

CHAPTER 13

It took some trips back and forth, but the first thing I did was take Robert's truck to get Courtney and Ricky. Then, Courtney drove the Hummer to the R family's farm. I did what I could to cover Robert's corpse with a seat cover from the truck, and dragged the others out of sight before the kids got out.

In the short drive, she had confirmed what I'd suspected. The folks that had attacked her, all lived within a good mile of each other. Cousins, plus the father/son combo were involved. Since they all went to the same church, they all knew each other well. When the food trucks had quit running, Robert's family would share with the church what they thought they could afford to until the crops came in. Two weeks ago, Randy had publicly called out the Redwood family. Yeah, they all had R first and last names, though Rebecca liked to be called Becky. A four-year-old rebel.

But at church, they'd accused the Redwood family of hoarding supplies. Robert had explained that he'd been preparing for bad times, but he hadn't prepared enough to carry the whole church through. He'd barely had enough for his own family, though none of them had believed him. He'd suggested they hunt until the corn and soy came in, but from what Rhonda told me (the mom), they had complained bitterly that the area had been hunted out. I looked at the massive rows of corn, almost ready for harvest, and couldn't help but wonder, what would happen to the many thousands and thousands of game animals that seemed to flock to farmland.

"Dick," Courtney said to get my attention, "come on out here."

I followed her. According to Rhonda, the supplies had been split up before Ben had dropped off the others, and then he had returned home. With neither the kids nor the mother knowing how to run the tractors and harvesters, nor anyone left alive to run them, it would all be done by hand. In the meantime, the stolen supplies were probably their best chance to survive the coming winter.

"I marked the map. We could both hit this one here and torch it, and when the other two come to investigate, we shoot them from ambush."

It was actually a good plan. The way the properties lined up, two of the cousins almost shared

188

THE DEVIL'S DUE

backyards with a third.

"How many of them have wives, kids?" I asked.

"Just this house," she said, pointing to the yellow smudge of a highlighted property. "Just a wife, no kids. Rhonda said the others have ex-wives, but none of them, nor the kids live with the families."

I'd let her do most of the talking with Rhonda. I'd slipped and scared the woman so badly that she'd tried to stab me. I knew that was a lot of people's first inclination to do to me, but I would never be around her long enough to gain her trust. I counted on Courtney getting through to her because she had a calming quality, and because she was a young woman. Plus, when Ricky had explained that she was my daughter, I hadn't corrected him. Courtney was about to start her snickering again when Becky asked her if she was Maggie.

She shot me a look and turned to the little girl, telling her that Maggie was my littlest daughter. She didn't correct her. Again, her words were not the full truth, yet they weren't lies. She was covering for me again. Even though she was also one of the many people whose first inclination had been to put a bullet in my head.

"We kill the men. If the woman was involved though…" the words trailed off as I recalled pulling the trigger.

I'd never killed a woman before today. Of all the death and destruction that I'd been a part of or caused, I'd never done that and it was tearing me up inside. I'd kicked the door in, seen the knife hand move, and instinct and training had taken over.

189

BOYD CRAVEN

From that distance, there was no way I could have missed. It was hard not to think about how little regard I'd given that woman when I'd woodenly pulled the trigger.

"Dick, Dick?" Courtney was waving a hand in my face.

"Yeah, sorry."

"What do you want me to do with the lady, if she was in on it?" she asked.

"Use your best judgement," I told her.

"I'm sorry, if it's any consolation."

"About what?"

"You having to do what you did today. Not the men, that was pretty much automatic. The wife of Ben."

I nodded. Once again, she could see right through me.

"If it has to happen, I won't lose sleep, not after what I heard Ben's wife tell Rhonda. They sounded like they should all be playing banjo music on some old movie set. Deliverance," I told her.

"Yeah, that." She spat the words. "I've got nothing against hillbillies and rednecks, but raping low-lifes like…" I was watching her hands and saw the cords of muscle in her arms bunch up as she made a fist.

I took her hand, much like Mel had taken mine, in what seemed like a lifetime ago, and smoothed her palm out. She resisted at first and then saw what I was doing.

"I hope it doesn't come to that, kiddo," I said, bumping the bottom of her chin with my free

190

thumb.

"Yeah, ok, *Dad*," she said in her snottiest voice.

I got it, her anger, her pain. How she'd championed taking care of the boy and later, the wife and daughter. She was still hurting and in pain. She was letting one emotion override the other. Grief and anger are two sides of the same coin in a lot of cases. What we were planning though, wasn't murder per se, but more along the lines of justice. We were taking back the stolen supplies, and making sure to put down anybody who'd be coming to avenge the deaths of the few I'd reaped today. It was killing for the sake of saving Rhonda's family from any more killing.

"Don't you Dad me," I said in a low voice. "I'll put you over my knee and spank you."

Her eyes got huge, and her mouth dropped open in shock. I knew it was a double entendre after what had almost happened between us during an unguarded moment, which was still a bit embarrassing, but I gambled on humor. She busted up laughing after a moment.

"Gotcha," I said, and walked toward the door to the side of the house.

"I didn't, you… It… GAH!"

"This old dog can still sling some snark," I said quietly as I knocked on the side door.

"Mr. Dick," Ricky said opening the door, "Momma and sissy are napping on the couch."

The kid was hesitating, unsure if he should let me in or not. I just wanted to say goodbye for now.

"Don't wake them. I'm going to go get your stuff

back, like the stuff we carried to the basement."

"There's a lot of it. Do you have a big enough spot for it in your van?" he asked, pointing to the Hummer.

"Yeah, I should be able to. Don't worry. Hey, do you know any of those folks?"

"Yeah," he said shyly, looking at his shoes. "They won't be coming back for my momma and sister, will they?"

"No, sweetie," Courtney said. "We're going to make sure of that, ok?"

"Ok. My mom and sis were so scared, and they cried and I guess they just got a little too sleepy. If they don't wake up when you come back, can you stay with me till they do?"

That got me, and I had to turn away as some dust blew into my eye. The kid was a thousand times better than he had been earlier, with a knot the size of a goose egg on the side of his head. He'd seen his father murdered and had had to consider that his mom and sister were gone as well. Or worse. Now, this six or seven-year-old dude was taking care of the ladies of the house.

"I will," I said.

He looked up and a smile tugged at the corners of his mouth. It was a grim, bitter day, but for him, it was over. All he had to do was keep on living, burying the horrors of the day in memory.

Ricky let the screen door close.

"You want to drive?" Courtney asked me.

"Doesn't matter."

As we got into the Hummer, Courtney busted

THE DEVIL'S DUE

up laughing again.

"What?"

"'Bend me over your knee'? You know, that isn't the most 'fatherly' comment I've heard this year."

I chuckled, "Yeah, figured it'd crack you up. Sorry if it was out of line."

"No, you just shocked the hell out of me. You kind of reminded me of how my dad was. So serious that you'd think a smile would crack his face, yet he would come up with wisecracks out of the blue, and I'd be left wondering if that sense of humor had always been there."

"I guess I have a little bit of a sense of humor, but don't let it get around. It might hurt my street cred."

She grinned and put the Hummer in gear. I sat back, checking my KSG and topping it off. I'd forgotten to earlier when the woman with the knife had been holding Rhonda. Still had a ton in the gun, yet I was out of habit. Maybe getting closer to the end would have me getting sloppy? I hoped not, sloppy got people killed and I'd almost had enough death. Still, three more souls would be joining their loved ones in Heaven and Hell shortly. Three more men, who would otherwise rob, murder, kidnap and destroy lives.

"We pulling into Ben's?" she asked.

"Yeah."

She parked the Hummer in the spot the trucks had been parked when I'd freed Rhonda, and killed the ignition. The map showed that the houses were within an easy walking distance. Not close enough that my shotgun blast could have been pinpointed, otherwise they would already be here, checking things out. Half to three quarters of a mile.

"Come on, follow me." I made my way toward the tangled mess at the back of the property.

"More corn?" she complained, but I could tell the whine was more out of habit than anything real.

"Until we hit the wooded fence line that borders the small cul-de-sac where the others live."

She grumbled once, but I could see her mind was elsewhere. She followed, about ten paces behind me, as I slowly worked my way through, using the tree line in the distance as a landmark. It would get me within spitting distance of the backyards of the subdivision. We were going about this plan somewhat sloppy. We didn't know for sure how many houses were occupied, but instead, were relying on the Humint (Human Intelligence) we'd heard from Rhonda. Most of the township had either left or stayed in place. Food and medicine were scarce and those who didn't have their own well, often died of waterborne illnesses.

It would have to be enough, though. I didn't want the men to discover what we'd done and mount a counterattack. We were still outnumbered, which seemed to be par for the course. Still, by having a plan, training and fighting from surprise and ambush, we'd been able to accomplish amazing feats and keep ourselves alive. These were the thoughts I dwelled on as I made it to the tree line and waited for Courtney to catch up.

"Which one is it?" I whispered, meaning the

THE DEVIL'S DUE

first house that we were going to hit and torch.

From this angle, it looked nothing like the map that we'd seen, and I was trying to get my bearings.

"That white house," she said, pointing.

That was what I was afraid of. We'd have to sneak through the backyards of three of the houses before we made it to the right one. I could tell which one it was, because it was the only white house I could see. The others were more of a gray or earth tones. Their yards were overgrown, the grass turning a shade of brown from a dry summer and early fall. Still, the white house had a large fishing boat beside it, and after looking at all of the dead grass I had an idea, if this was where the flare gun had come from. I still hadn't figured out what they were trying to do with it, but I wasn't about to sit them down and ask them either.

"Grass and corn is too dry to light the house. Let's check the boat first, then do the dirty deeds," I whispered.

She nodded and we set out. Moving along the outer fence lines was nerve wracking. Every darkened window could hold a sniper, every door could have men stacked up, ready to come boiling out with gunfire or worse, attack dogs. I kept these happy thoughts running on a loop as my adrenaline started pumping, making my ears and eyes seem to pulse with the heavier blood flow. A small tension headache was forming. I didn't give it any thought as I kept crawling, only checking on Courtney once. She was following my movements, her carbine pointed more or less toward the empty houses in an army style crawl, even lower to the ground than I was.

I stopped at the edge of the last house before we made it to the white one. This was the first house we'd encountered, where there seemed to be light flickering at a window. A candle or lamp perhaps. I looked up to the sky and was surprised to see that it had started to get dark. With that happy thought my stomach rumbled, reminding me that the entire day was almost over and I'd yet to eat. We still had too much work to do, so I ignored that and watched the windows as I made my way over to the fishing boat.

On the right side, where the driver, pilot or whatever you called them sat, was a fire extinguisher. Clipped next to it was a hand held air horn. The kind people buy to use at stadium games and give other people big fucking headaches. I unclipped it and put it in my left dump pouch. That being done, we got into a crouch and pushed our way to the front door through the overgrown lawn and scrub, that had probably been growing here before the EMP.

"Want me to knock?" Courtney asked, one eyebrow raised.

"Knock? Really?" What was she thinking?

She undid the top button of her BDU top, took her hat off and shook her hair out. Well shit, I had to look somewhere else for a second.

"Yeah, just be ready,"

She slung her carbine, pulled her pistol with her right hand, and held it behind her back. She boldly walked up to the front door and banged on it with her left hand and stepped back. Immediately, we could hear footsteps pounding toward the front door.

"Lucy, I told you, I don't have more milk—"

"Avon lady," Courtney told him.

Those were the last words cut off by a .45 in the heart. The report was loud, but the man never registered the fact that Courtney wasn't Lucy. Oh shit, was she the woman from the house behind him? I fumbled for the air horn as Courtney pushed him inside and we shut the door. It took us a minute to clear the house and already we could hear some shouts from the backyard. It had to be the other two men from the raid, asking if everything was all right.

"Give me the horn," Courtney said.

I did and she sprinted toward the front door and started depressing the button. The horn blasted the mostly silent twilight into a loud raucous. She held it down for a long note and then started honking it with short one second blasts and then dropped it. She still had her .45 in her other hand and took position just to the left of the door. When it opened, she would be just out of sight. Outside, I could hear two men calling to each other and the sound of them moving through the uncut yard toward the porch.

"…Probably drunk and shot himself in the leg…" one voice said as the doorknob wiggled.

"He didn't lock it, did he?"

Courtney let out another blast. It startled me

and she shrugged her shoulders, dropped the canister on the ground, and took the .45 in a two-handed grip.

"It sticks," a deeper voice said and the handle turned and with a bump, the door popped open.

The first thing they would see was the corpse of their dear departed friend. The second thing would be me rising from where I was crouched in the shadows, at the back of an afghan-covered couch.

When it kicked off, one man went to a pistol holstered in one hand and another started bringing up an old side-by-side shotgun as if in slow motion. I don't know who shot first, me or Courtney, but both men were hit multiple times by each of us. They fell where they had tried coming in the doorway, wedging themselves in place and in death.

"That was too easy," I said, reaching into the dump pouch to start reloading the four slugs I'd just expended.

When we were done, I would make my loadout more along the lines of what I normally would do; alternate slugs with buckshot.

"Dick, I'll be back," Courtney said as I was pumping the last shell in the KSG's inner magazine.

"Want me to watch your back?" I asked her.

"I got this. Either she's going to be a problem, or she's not."

I reached out and grabbed the corpse holding the pistol and pulled, making the other fall into the doorway, his head almost up the man I was dragging's ass.

"Hurry back and be safe," I said. "I'm going to

THE DEVIL'S DUE

find the supplies they took here and meet you outside. Give me a whistle as you come, so I know it's you."

"You got it." And she was gone.

CHAPTER 14

There was a lot of stuff in the house. Enough that I forgot about the coppery metallic scent of blood, the disgusting smell of loose bowels, and just stared. I'd seen people with some stuff, but this couldn't have all been taken from the R family's house. It was just too much. I started pulling boxes out of a walk-in pantry just off the kitchen and set them on the table. A lot of the items had been bought locally, but there were things that just didn't fit… At least, not what I was expecting. Some of the food had labels in Cyrillic, like nothing I'd seen around here.

In the bedroom, there was another find. An M249 SAW leaned up against the wall. Military weapons and foreign food? I could see the preppers' food easily enough, buckets of wheat, beans, rice and dehydrated foods... but cases upon cases of MREs that I knew to be Russian surplus? What the hell had we walked into?

I heard a woman scream, and I grabbed the SAW as I made my way out of the house. I pulled the charging handle and saw that the belt had been already fed and a live round was in the chamber there. I hurried more than I liked to, visions of Courtney being slowly skinned alive, filling my brain. I rushed around the corner to see Courtney stalking toward me, a white cloth-wrapped bundle in her hands. Tears were streaming down her cheeks, and she ignored the thin brunette screaming bloody murder behind her. My eyes got huge as the cloth bundle was put into my left hand, my right barely holding the SAW.

It moved, and a baby's squall startled me so badly I almost dropped it. Instead, I dropped the SAW onto the soft overgrown lawn as the woman screamed again.

"He did it for my baby, and you killed him!" The woman's sobs were so extreme that her whole body shook.

Courtney was also on the verge of all-out sobs herself. The baby in my hands made a noise again, and I moved the blanket off its face. As soon as the waning light touched its skin, it quieted and looked up at me with big brown eyes. I reached in and touched its perfect skin with one scarred finger. Soft, but hot. Fevered, even.

"Lucy?" I asked as Courtney shot me a look and put her .45 in her holster. She picked up the SAW I'd set down beside me.

"Ye..Yes..." She kept crying.

"Your husband, was he one of the men who came over here to check on this guy?" I said, pointing to the house.

She nodded.

"Your husband and these men killed a farmer down the road, stole his supplies, and kidnapped his wife and daughter."

She fell to her knees, her hands ripping at the grass as she shook her head.

"We had to make sure they didn't go back and kill the woman and children," I told her, never having been in a situation like this that I could ever remember.

"She's sick, and if she don't get more milk in her, she's going to di… di…"

She couldn't say it. Obviously, the child was sick. I could feel it now, the heat radiating through the thin cotton blanket it was swaddled in.

"Did you know they were going to do some killing?" I asked her.

She was too pathetic to be a monster who would go along with something like this. I wanted to see if she knew beforehand though, or what her thoughts were. Maybe it would make it easier to figure out what to do. For as tough as Courtney talked, she was as wrecked as the woman was and my heart was breaking over all of this, for the second or third time in one day. Why couldn't things be black and white? Good guys, bad guys… not screaming, crying wives and sick babies. No more dead husbands,

THE DEVIL'S DUE

who had been playing in the barn with their sons, trying to teach them some new skillsets.

"No, they promised me that they were going to ask him if we could get some milk. He's got goats in the back pasture, and she's been so sick, she hasn't been nursing and now I'm not producing…"

"How long has it been?" I asked her, looking at the baby.

"Off and on for a week and a half. I got her to take a bottle, but it was mostly broth and water. She's going to die if I can't—"

"Dick," Courtney's words were quiet, despite the hitching in her chest.

"Go get the Hummer."

* * *

"Mr. Dick, my mom is up, want me to get her?" Ricky said as I walked up to the screen door.

I looked back and Courtney was sitting beside Lucy and the baby in the rear seats. I turned back to Ricky and nodded. He took off with a drunken gait from the concussion and I could hear some murmured words, and then Rhonda came out.

"Is it done?" she asked, her eyes red.

What is it with women crying that killed me? If I could figure out how to turn that part of my brain off, I could live life a lot easier.

"Mostly," I said, and made a motion with my hand.

The door opened and I turned, watching with Rhonda as Lucy and Courtney stepped out, Lucy holding the baby.

"Is that Lucy McCord?" she asked me without turning her head.

"Yeah, apparently, she has a one-and-a-half-month old baby."

"Why is she…"

"Ma'am," Lucy said as she walked up, her voice stronger than the sobbing woman I'd met half an hour ago. "I'm very sorry for the actions of my husband and his kin. I didn't want this to happen to him, and to mine as well…"

She stumbled and Courtney caught her shoulder before she could go over.

"My baby is sick. He was supposed to ask if we could buy, barter or get some goat milk, so I can…"

"Oh, honey," Rhonda flew past me as she ran to the woman and embraced her warmly.

For a moment, I thought the baby would be squished between the mass of female flesh and raging hormones. So much so that I took a step back and felt little hands wrap around my leg. I looked down and little Becky was holding onto my leg. I felt somebody put arms around my waist and turned to see Ricky was holding on, either for support or to make sure I didn't turn and run, probably like he wanted to do. Courtney took the baby from between them when it started squalling and walked toward me, so the women could embrace and talk.

They were so close, it almost looked like more than it was, but their words were both comforting, forgiving, and too much.

"Do you two rascals know if your mom has a

baby bottle?" Courtney asked Ricky.

"Yeah, 'Becks still has one now and then."

"Do not," she said softly.

"Momma has one on the sink strainer with the lid thing," he shot back.

"Milk?"

"In the basement cooler," Rebecca told me.

I felt two sets of hands let me go, and then both of my hands were grabbed by their smaller ones.

"Come on, I'll show you."

I looked over my shoulder to see Courtney smiling at me, despite the tears in her eyes.

* * *

"Give me Doc," I said into the radio, once I got through to Steve's people.

I'd set up a shortwave set and dialed in the frequency that they monitored.

"Wait one," a voice said, and I could almost hear the sneer in the operator's voice.

"Doesn't look like they forgive all that quickly," Courtney said from beside me.

She was looking exhausted. She'd bottle-fed the baby once and had been refilling it when Lucy had taken over, and had told Courtney that the baby needed a burp or she would puke for sure. The baby would probably puke anyway, even I knew that, with what little knowledge I had of babies.

"No," I said.

"Doc, here," his voice came out of the speakers quicker than I could have imagined.

He must have been in the bunker already.

"Doc, sick baby girl. One-and-a-half-months old. Fever, worse than normal diarrhea, vomiting and a cough. What do you think?" I asked.

"Bad water issues where you're at?"

I thought on that, and then nodded and answered, "Rumors of contaminated water as the area had a big die off. It's probably been a month or so since then," I said, looking at Rhonda who nodded.

"You have that kit I gave your girl?"

"You gave them what?" another voice cut in on the transmission.

"Yes, I do," I said as Courtney nodded.

"Stay off the line, I'm talking," Doc admonished whomever it was who had interrupted him.

"We're talking to Steve and Jamie later," the voice said and then was gone.

I could hear a sigh and then Doc spoke, "Courtney, write this down."

He gave her the dosage of a shot to be given to the baby. With it being so young, there was no chance of getting it to swallow a pill, and making a liquid suspension that the infant could keep down was probably beyond our means. As it was, we had some broad spectrum injectable antibiotics. She repeated his instructions back twice to make sure, and he said she had it correct. Courtney handed the handset back to me and went outside where her gear bag was.

"Doc, what're the baby's chances?" I asked him.

"Is it eating?" he asked me.

"Almost six ounces in one sitting."

THE DEVIL'S DUE

"How long has it been sick?" he asked.

"Week and a half. Her mom was getting frantic because her own milk dried up. Luckily, a family around here has a goat in milk and…"

"Good, good. Sounds like the biggest part of the danger is over then. Clean water or milk, that injection and some prayers."

"That's it?" I asked.

"The baby probably is going to beat it on its own, as long as it doesn't die of dehydration. Listen, do you know how to purify water?" His voice was raspy and it crackled at the end.

"Yeah, I've got tabs, but boil, bleach, filter with sand and charcoal… Listen, bad water won't be a problem anymore."

The R family had a windmill, and the well had always tasted fresh and clear of any contaminates.

"Good, well, if that's all you need, I've got a broken jaw to heal shut."

"Broken jaw?" I asked.

"Yeah, whoever it was that Jamie threatened to throw out, got mouthy with Steve. You know what a jealous, overprotective bastard the sheriff is."

"That I do," I said laughing.

"He'll be on the broth diet for a while, himself. Maybe I'll even give him some of Ensure I stockpiled for myself… with a little Milk of Magnesia mixed in."

I laughed, "You're an ornery one, Doc. I'm glad to have met you."

"Wish I could say the same. As much as I like you, Dick, part of me wonders if you can keep on

207

dealing out violence and death without it breaking you. I'd think about that, and I'll pray for you, my friend."

His words somewhat mirrored what I'd been thinking earlier and I had to admit, he was right.

"I was thinking of retiring to a farm myself. Raising some chickens, playing cards with the neighbors, and hanging up my guns."

Doc chuckled before going on, "That all sounds good and well… but if you're a fan of spaghetti westerns, there's a Clint Eastwood movie you might like… An old gunfighter hangs up his guns— till trouble finds him."

"What happens then?" I asked, despite myself.

"He becomes a gunfighter again. You're a lot like him, you know. You're a shit magnet. Trouble seems to follow you, even though you don't want it to. You were put on Earth for a reason. I'd like to hope it is to confront and fight evil at every turn, but it isn't a life for everyone. I wish you a quiet retirement, though, Dick. I hope you find contentment and happiness."

I chewed on that a long while.

"Still there?" Doc asked.

"Yeah," I said and paused again. "Thanks, Doc, you've got great bedside manner. I'll make sure to stay in touch, so you and the men with the white coats and butterfly nets can scoop me up when it's time."

"Bedside manner? Shit, son, that's like trying to pick up a turd from the clean end. Ain't gonna happen. You just keep you and your girl safe till you get

208

THE DEVIL'S DUE

home. Give Miss Mary and Maggie my best."

"Thanks, Doc," I said.

"Doc, Out."

I heard the baby suddenly let out a loud wail and murmuring female voices. I tossed the handset in the front seat of the Hummer and went inside the farmhouse. Courtney was carrying a slim black case and passed me on her way out to take it back to the Hummer.

"Baby didn't like the shot," Becky said.

I looked at the ladies who were in recliners across from each other. The kids were sitting on a loveseat facing an old stone fireplace, and other than the kitchen chairs, the couch looked to be the safest place to sit to wait on Courtney. There was a lot of gear and supplies to get from the houses, but it was getting late and I'd only eaten an MRE out of desperation.

"Here, you hold her," Lucy said, handing me the baby, who was still making crying noises.

I held her up and then pulled the blanket from her face, my fingers supporting her head. She quieted and looked at me. Then I put her head on my shoulder and leaned back, rubbing the back of the small lump of baby. I could feel its body relaxing and then the soft regular breathing in my ear. My eyes drifted shut as I let the day's events wash through my head. My thinking slowed, and I felt somebody prop my feet up on a stool. Then a heavy blanket was placed over me, and I realized somebody was taking the baby from my arms.

"Shhhh," Courtney whispered to me, "We'll do

209

the rest tomorrow."

I felt her head rest on my shoulder and I took a deep breath to say something, but I must have drifted off.

CHAPTER 15

It took us two days to move all of the supplies. The first house we investigated, we hit a major jackpot. Apparently, the man who had lived there, at one point had worked for the DHS and had partially looted a stockpile before going AWOL. He didn't have any family other than cousins and uncles, yet he'd never once mentioned that he was sitting on more food than Rhonda's family. We even found a couple cans of formula at the bottom of the pantry. The real shocker was the cans of ammo; 5.56 in loose rounds and a couple cans of linked rounds for the SAW.

We kept the SAW and the ammo for it, but when we found the older style M16s we gave those, the mags for them and all the ammunition to Rhonda. Courtney gave them a primer on how to load, fire and clean the guns. I could have taught them, but I'd found out something about myself a long time ago: I may be pretty good at what I do, but when it comes to teaching, I suck. Courtney seemed to have a natural knack for teaching, so I let her do it.

Also the food. It wasn't as good as Steve's cook would have made, but I couldn't tell them that. The two ladies had decided to throw in together, and they treated us to a big home-cooked meal. I didn't understand how them coming together had happened, but maybe it had something to do with now being widowed parents, trying to survive the apocalypse together. More power to them. Still, I spent two days as a draft horse, moving supplies to the old farm.

I didn't know what they were going to do about the corn, but that wasn't my concern. The little boy, Ricky, got better a lot faster than I'd expected, though. Nausea plagued him off and on for the first day, but by the end of the second day, he was mostly better. He clung to me when he could, and I recognized part of it. He'd lost his father, and even though I never would be him, I was at least somebody he trusted, that he felt safe around. It had been like that with the kids of mine, back in Chicago.

"When are we going to go?" Courtney asked me, as I checked things in my bag for the eleventh time.

"In the morning, I think. I'm going to hang out here for a while, and try to see if I can get anybody on the horn from my area back home."

"Where are we headed, exactly?"

THE DEVIL'S DUE

Good question, I guessed I hadn't talked about that much. Simply saying 'Arkansas' had seemed good enough at the time, but we were getting close now. Southeast for a good twelve hours, during normal traffic patterns, but there was nothing normal about these days. So two days travel, maybe?

"Russellville," I told her.

"Huh, ok."

She reached across me and pulled out the maps, kicking back while I tried the radio. The heat from the day felt good inside the Hummer. It wasn't oppressive, but it was heavy, like a warm bath after waking up sore. I turned the radio off and leaned back, knowing I was getting sleepy.

"I'll make sure everything is topped off. The ladies said we can fill everything up with their big tank for the tractor."

"Ok," I told her, drifting.

* * *

I knew I was dreaming. The colors were too bright, too vivid. The sounds had a quality to them that seemed off, flat.

I was walking up to the gate that separated the drive to the farm from the country road. No neighbors as far as the eye could see. A sign had been hand painted, and probably just propped up against the gate. It had fallen, so I leaned down and picked up a 2'x3' piece of plywood that had letters made out of black spray paint.

'Plague. Do not enter. Sickness and Death.'

213

BOYD CRAVEN

I dropped the sign, not wanting to think about it and used my hands to lever myself over the top of the tubular gate until my boots hit the ground on the other side, making my ankles scream with a brief flash of pain. Normally in dreams, I didn't feel the pain, but clearly this wasn't a regular dream. I decided not to fight it too much, but just see where the journey took me.

As if I was watching myself in a movie, I moved down the gravel drive, which became circular and twisty as it wound its way to the bottom of the valley. Trees obscured the clearing where the farmhouse sat. I had been there a time or two, and I remembered the red colored t-111 plywood exterior and metal roof. The house had been remodeled so many times, it was hard to tell where the old moonshiners tarpaper shack had been extended into a modern residence. Well, modern if you still lived in the boondocks in the thirties and forties.

"No," I said, my words making steam rise in the crisp autumn air.

As I rounded the last curve, I could see no smoke coming from the chimney. They would have run the fireplace at this temp, I was sure. Maybe there was some truth to the sign after all. I started to jog, not feeling the impacts in my knees like I would have, if it was real life. As I hurried, I took in the unkempt appearance of the homestead. All the machinery to keep the farm running was overturned, some disassembled near the barn. There were scorched areas in the hay field where something had burned and the sickly smell of death

214

THE DEVIL'S DUE

grew deeper, the closer I got to the house.

I hesitated at the door, more afraid of what I'd find than anything else. I'd been gone so long, so far from here, that last step, a knock, seemed more difficult than I'd expected. The door opened and I almost fell back in shock. James stood there, gore smeared down the sides of his face and his filed teeth glinting with a red tint as he smiled at me.

"Come in, come in, Mike. We've all been waiting for you."

James was mad. He'd suffered a brain injury in real life and had turned into a different man, one I'd had to kill. I'd been exonerated when the truth had come out and I'd almost lost my retirement over the fiasco, but this had the quality of a fevered nightmare, and I knew not to take anything too seriously. Still, my heart hammered in my chest as I stepped across the threshold and followed him.

"Why do you call me Mike?" I asked, wondering if my nightmare was twisting the death of both of my friends.

"Oh, it's just a dream. Or is it? Besides," he paused and turned, opening his arms as if to say "tada!", "he's dead, she's dead, they're all dead. Down here, it's all we have. Nightmares, bad dreams and our own personal devils to face."

I looked and even though I knew it was coming, I saw the corpses. Mary's parents had been sitting side by side on the couch when their throats had been cut. Mary was half off the couch when a knife had been buried in her back between her shoulder blades, and Maggie... I just saw a pair of legs, al-

215

ready mottled in color from death and decay. I was breaking. I wanted to scream incoherently, but I was rooted to the spot. The vision of their deaths was the worst thing I could have—

"See, down here in Hell, it really doesn't matter what I call you, does it, sweetheart?"

He came for me, the filed points of the teeth flashing—

* * *

"Dick!!!!!"

I was thrown forward until the restraints of the seatbelt pulled on me painfully, almost crushing the air out of my lungs. As fast as I was flung forward, the sudden stop pushed me back into the seat. My heart was rushing itself into a stroke or heart attack. I looked around and wiped the moisture off my face and saw Courtney in the driver's seat, pulling off a pair of NVGs.

"Dick, are you ok?"

"Where... what?"

"You were having a nightmare," she said. "I was worried you were going to stroke out."

I felt for the release, and when I found it, I threw the belt off and opened the door, stumbling outside. I started retching and dry heaving on the side of the road, my entire body cramped up, and only when I finally let out a wet burp, did my stomach settle again. I stood, wiping my mouth with my sleeve and looked around. Daylight was starting to filter across the horizon, but it was pretty dark still.

216

THE DEVIL'S DUE

Early morning.

"Where are we?" I asked, getting back in the Hummer, feeling as weak as a kitten.

"We're between Pittsburg and Joplin," she said, giving me a wan smile.

"Missouri?" I asked, trying to remember the geography.

"Yeah, about to cross into Arkansas."

"I thought we were going to leave in the morning?"

"I was too nerved up. I was going to wake you up soon, anyway. I'm getting tired and I've used two of the four fuel cans to keep this thing topped off. Figured you could decide if you wanted to push on or not."

My brain almost skipped a gear. I'd fallen asleep and she'd let me, buckling me in and just driving. Granted, she'd had the NVGs so we could drive without lights, but that was damned dangerous and she didn't have somebody to watch her six, and the way those cannibals had boiled out of the darkness and…

"Hey, don't be mad. I heard on the radio, some folks talking. FEMA came through this entire corridor. They cleared the roads going north and south, and everyone that they can move has moved. There's a big fight in Texas and this is going to be used as a north-south corridor in a month. Nobody is around here, Dick."

"I know," I said, having heard a lot of that myself, a day prior, "It's just damned dangerous. What if somebody was driving up behind us? You didn't have enough sets of eyes…"

"Dick," she said softly, "we've walked, ridden bikes, driven trucks and Hummers. We've been attacked by dogs, cannibals, crazy religious townspeople, and the federal government. We're still alive. We've kind of had a crazy time, a crazy ride, and a crazy life, lately. I figured we might as well go with what's working."

"The crazy?" I asked her sarcastically.

In a serious voice, she said, "Exactly. Besides, once you started dreaming about coming home, you talked almost nonstop. I thought you were awake and were trying to keep me awake, but then you started having nightmares."

"They were all dead," I said.

"In your nightmares. Besides, I don't think rolling up to them in the dark would be the best way to be reintroduced to your family. This way, we're about two hundred miles away. We can make it there before dinner, if you can help me refill the tanks."

"I can do that," I said, stretching.

She was right; crazy had been somewhat of a hallmark of mine and it was what went best. It was when I over-planned things that Murphy would show up and kick me in the balls. This gamble, so far, had paid off well, and I could tell we weren't on one of the major loops around a big city. The kid had done all right, and I shot her a smile. We had come to a stop about forty feet away from a semi, so I felt around till I found the two empty cans and put them on the still-warm asphalt, and then fished

218

THE DEVIL'S DUE

around till I found the barrel pump.

It was something I'd snagged from the farm. It was a pump that sat on top of a 55-gallon barrel. One end went into the fuel, the other end into a tank. It didn't just pump fuel, but that's what we were going to use it for. It was kind of like a wind-up power syphon. Tucking that under my arm, I started walking. I heard the crunch behind me and saw Courtney following along slowly. When I got to the semi, I knocked on the large chromed fuel tank behind the driver's door and was rewarded with a hollow sound about ¾ the way up. It had fuel, and more than we could carry.

Sometimes, I thought I was luckier than I had any right to be, but I never said that out loud. Murphy, of Murphy's law, loved it when I got too happy or spoke aloud about how well my luck was going. He loved nothing more than to come out of the woodwork and screw up my life. Once it had shrapnel from an IED, another time it was the trap we'd walked into while under sniper fire… or the time I had gotten clean for a short period of time and Mary had said…

What had she said? I popped the top off the fuel tank, got the can in place, and started pumping. As the fuel started flowing, I thought harder. The memory was close to the surface, but I wasn't sure if it was more dream or memory. It was like I was watching an old black and white movie without the sound. Mary was looking at me, pity in her eyes as I showed her the token. Thirty days clean. It was one of the first times I'd been at Salina's clinic, and had just gotten over a blood infection from dirty needles. She'd told me, "We've been here before, I know you're trying," or something like that.

She hadn't looked at me with any of the warmth that I would have expected. Maybe that was why it was so hard to remember. She'd looked at me like she would look at the neighbors' twelve-year-old, who'd been caught trying to sneak a peek through the curtains. Disgust, disinterest. Was I really that much of a cad?

"Don't overflow it," Courtney yelled.

I flipped her off and got the second can going. Mary... when was the last time I had seen her? When she was leaving me, I knew that, but it seemed like there was one other time now. Had I gone to Arkansas? I remembered a bus ride, a hospital. A doctor had been there. Memories swam into focus. I was laying on a bed in restraints. Not like the one Skinner had me in, but more so that I didn't lash out and hurt someone by accident. Rehab?

"He's going to get better, isn't he?" a child asked.

As much as I tried to remember, I couldn't see them, but I recognized that it was Maggie's voice.

"It's in God's hands now. He has to stay on his meds, or he's going to lose it again." That was Mary, and I could see her talking to someone behind me, probably Maggs.

I tried to remember the rest, but it was gone. I stopped the pump and put the lid on the second can. I walked both full ones to the back and strapped them in. When that was done, Courtney pulled the Hummer up closer.

220

THE DEVIL'S DUE

"Excuse me sir, I need half a tank of unleaded," she said through my open window.

"Smartass." I motioned her forward with my hands until she was close enough for me to get the hose into the fuel port.

I took the cap off and started the process over.

"You look like you're still dreaming," Courtney said as I turned the handle.

"Memories. Something triggered from my dream," I told her truthfully.

"What was it? Mary and Maggie?"

"Yeah. I was thinking about the last time I saw them in Chicago… and then realized that I've seen them once more."

"Oh yeah? Where was that?"

"In a hospital somewhere," I said listening to the gurgle of diesel, knowing I would overflow it if I wasn't careful.

"You don't remember?"

"No, not really. So much of my life… There's huge chunks of time that are just gone. Other memories are like watching an old silent film. You can see what's going on, but without subtitles or voices, you're lost."

"Is it part of… you know…"

I knew. My broken mental process.

"I think so," I said softly.

"Do you think you're ever going to be a hundred percent again?"

For a moment I wanted to be angry, but of all people, I realized that she was asking because she truly cared.

BOYD CRAVEN

"I don't know. There's medicine and therapy that I was supposed to stick with."

"Then the world went to hell," Courtney said.

"No, I went to hell long before the world did. It's my fault."

I was pretty sure I'd told Jamie and Mel my story, how I'd lost Mary and Maggs, and my fell into addiction, but I didn't want to rehash it with Courtney if I hadn't. Even those memories were starting to get hazy for me. Almost like what I'd imagined Early Onset Dementia to feel like. Then again, I knew that massive depression and PTSD could cause long and short term memory loss. Funny, of all things, I could remember that.

"Don't worry, we'll fix this, all of it, today."

"Promise?" I asked, a note of hope in my voice.

She laughed at me. The blonde-haired blue-eyed brat laughed at me. I was about to give her some snark when I heard the gurgle at the top of the fueling port, so I quickly pulled the hose and quit pumping before I overflowed the fuel. I capped the truck's chromed tank, as well as the Hummer's, before throwing the barrel pump in the back. The smell of fuel wafted up, but I didn't care. Two hundred miles.

"Hey, McGigglepants, move over. I'm driving."

"I'm sorry, it's just…"

"Don't make me—"

"Don't!" Her guffaws were loud enough to scare crows up that'd been picking at something further up the road.

I opened the driver's door and bumped her with

222

my hip until she crawled over the middle and into the passenger seat. I got in and slammed the door, moving the seat back and checking the mirrors.

"Do you need the NVGs?"

"I know where we are," I said, noticing the mile marker and sign in the distance.

"So, we're close?"

"Closer than I've ever been," I said, and put it into gear.

CHAPTER 16

Two hundred miles. Six hours roughly by my count. It would feel like a lifetime. Still, I drove like a robot while Courtney sleepily watched all around us. The only slip up we had was when we started toward the outskirts of Fort Smith. Two cars were pushed nose-to-nose blocking the highway, and three men were pointing rifles in our direction. Courtney had taken the SAW and put up the tripod on the roof, and when the men saw that, plus the military style Hummer, they pushed the cars apart and walked across the highway with their hands and rifles pointed straight up.

Courtney kept the M249 aimed their way until we were half a mile past. I didn't know if they were blocking off a small town from people, raiding those they could slow down, or forcing people to

THE DEVIL'S DUE

listen to their spiel about Jesus and the second coming of Christ. I didn't care, I barely noticed. I recognized the tunnel vision that I was falling into. It was the same thing that'd happened, during every combat action I'd ever been in. Knowing that, I kept my breathing steady, kept the adrenaline from making me shiver and shake, and just kept on going, trusting Courtney to handle any external threats.

"We're close now," I said as she popped back inside from the top hatch.

Our Hummer didn't have a turret, but that hadn't prevented Courtney from donning some clear goggles and letting the hot wind blow her hair back. She'd said she felt like Tank Girl, something I'd have to ask Maggie about. I felt out of touch with pop culture, but this one seemed like I'd ought to have remembered it.

"How close?" she asked.

"Inside twenty minutes," I told her, turning off onto a side street.

We'd been cruising almost nonstop. Instead of keeping the fuel topped off in the Hummer, I'd let it run down, to the point where we'd have to stop soon. Problem was, the rural area we were in, had people drawn to the roadside by the sound of the diesel engine. Many of them were gaunt, but their stomachs weren't bloated from starvation. More like, regular meals weren't a normal thing. So, finding a quiet-looking spot where the trees covered both sides of the road, I pulled to the middle and stopped, killing the motor.

It ticked loudly as it started cooling. I swatted

225

at a lazy mosquito that floated in through the open window, intent on dive bombing the side of my neck and got out. Courtney followed.

"I'll cover you," she said, hoisting the SAW.

"You're getting attached to that thing, aren't you?" I asked her.

"It's got a whole lot of boom in one package."

"Here's a tip for ya, Courtney, that thing is seventeen pounds when it's empty, and add five pounds for a string of shells. How many reloads do you want to carry?"

"Twenty-two pounds plus reloads doesn't sound like a lot."

"Plus your pack, your sidearm, plus your medical supplies, plus…"

"You were about to make a fat joke, weren't you," she said pointedly.

"Nope," I said grinning, "but I'd like to see a lady who's a buck twenty carry her own body weight, holding a machine gun that makes Arnold looks like a badass in *Commando*."

"Was that an old eighties movie?"

"Yeah, why?"

"I thought so. I've heard of it. I think my grandpa watched those old eighties flicks."

"You making an old joke?" I asked her as I started filling the Hummer from the first fuel can.

"Fair's fair, besides, I'm one-fifteen, not one-twenty."

"Oh, excuuuuuuuuuuuuuse me."

The banter was lighthearted and we were both being quiet, almost whispering. So I was surprised

226

THE DEVIL'S DUE

when I heard someone wolf whistle. I turned, look-ing while setting the now empty can down.

"I got eyes, Dick, keep on going. It's just a kid on a BMX on the hill to your left."

"Ma'am, are you with the Army people?" His voice floated out over the still hot humid air.

"No, just helping a friend get home to his fam-ily."

"Why you got the fancy clothes and machine gun?" he asked, riding closer.

I cursed quietly, knowing that I probably wasn't going to be able to finish fueling. We would have to do what we could, go, and hope for the best. Still, he didn't look like a threat, appeared unarmed, and only had eyes for Courtney.

"It's amazing what you find lying about. My old clothes got gross."

"Oh," he said, coming to a stop about thirty feet away from us on the dirt road.

"Mister, I don't mean no harm," he said to me.

I nodded and capped the second empty fuel can, then grabbed a third. "What's your name, kid?"

"Russell, sir," he said.

"Can you tell me if you know the Pershings?"

"Miss Mary and Miss Maggie? Why, sue, all us guys know Maggie."

I gritted my teeth and resisted the urge to pull my pistol out until he said, "She's the one who's been teaching some of us younger guys to shoot. Said her daddy taught her when she was a little'un. My big brother thinks he's gonna marry her someday, but I think he's full of it. She ain't old enough, and she

227

thinks he smells like a cow's ass."

Courtney snorted, and for half a second I kept pouring fuel till I met the kid's eyes.

"Oh, excuse the language, ma'am," he said to Courtney, "but she don't like my brother none. He's really a jerk. Do you know them?"

"You could say that," I told him, straining to keep the third fuel can steady while I was pouring.

It became taxing after a while, and unless there was a semi somewhere, this refuel would be what we had till we found more diesel.

"She told me about her daddy once. Soldier who got shot up in one of the wars, a few years before the EMP. You know him?"

His eyes were boring into mine and I nodded. "You could say that." A smile broke across my face.

"Oh good, I'm glad I didn't try to steal that kiss at the dance two nights…"

I dropped the gas can and started walking toward him. Courtney put up a hand and pushed me in the chest. I turned and got the fuel can and capped it, before what little was left covered the dirt road.

"He's just a kid," she said and looked over her shoulder where we both could see him riding away, like his ass was on fire and his hair was catching. "I think he finally took the hint. Hopefully, he doesn't ruin your surprise."

"Oh damn, I didn't think of that," I said, putting the can in the back and the cap on the Hummer.

"Want me to drive?"

"No, I got this," I told her, wiping my hands on

my pants. They stank like fuel.

"Let's git'er done," she said in a hokey, country-sounding voice.

"Was that a nineties or a millennial reference?" I asked her blandly.

"Yeah, Larry the Cable Guy…"

"Kids," I said, firing up the Hummer and putting it into gear.

* * *

"Is that the gate?" Courtney asked.

"Yeah," I said, my heart rate through the roof.

My mouth suddenly was dry, and for the first time in weeks, I desperately wanted a drink. Not water, but a good shot of bourbon, whiskey, vodka, something. Something to give me courage, something to—

"Somebody's coming up the driveway."

I turned the Hummer off and got out. I didn't lean on the gate but instead, leaned on the bumper and waited. The thing that scared me more than cannibals came into sight and I froze solid, every muscle clenching. A quad was racing into sight, ridden by a man wearing a red-checkered shirt, with steel gray hair that was longer than I remembered, flowing over his shoulders. A permanent scowl would be the first thing a stranger noticed, but for me, it was the .44. He had always carried a Smith and Wesson .44 Magnum, and his Dirty Harry gun was on his hip. He slid to a stop five feet away from his side of the gate, killed the motor, and stepped off.

"What do you want?"

My mouth opened and closed and I tried again, "Hey, Pops. How's everyone doing?"

He spit, and then looked me over again. Recognition lit his features, but instead of smiling, the scowl deepened.

"Ma's as ornery as ever. Mary's making a pumpkin pie from some mix we canned last year, and Maggie is down at the creek with some boy. Teaching him how to shoot."

"Maggie's where?" I asked.

"Don't worry, this boy is about eight-years-old. No need to get your long johns all twisted up. Who's this lady with ya?"

"This is Courtney. She's… a friend of mine."

"A girlfriend, a druggie friend?"

"Excuse me?" Courtney asked, clearly horrified.

"A druggie? You know, somebody who takes too many pills, smokes meth, injects shit in their veins. You some kind of druggie?"

"No, and I'm not his girlfriend, either." Her scowl matched the old man's in equal amounts of disgust and horror.

"Oh, just a friend, huh?"

"He saved me from a gang of men who were going to sell me," she said, her eyes filling with tears, and her hands began to shake with anger.

I was glad she didn't have the SAW handy. Oh boy, was I glad. The old man did that to me, too.

"Oh well, might as well let you in then. You been clean?" he asked me.

THE DEVIL'S DUE

"Yeah," I lied, not wanting to count the forced injections by Skinner. Thankfully, he'd been out of my dreams lately.

"Hold on, let me unhook the batteries," he said, and walked to the thick brush, fiddled with something, and then motioned for me as he opened the gate.

"Want me to leave the Hummer here?" I asked him.

"Naw, drive through. I'll hook the 'lectricity up after you come in. Just drive real slow like, so I can keep up with ya, or I'll use this old hog leg on ya," he said, patting the .44.

"Yes, sir," I said as I got in the Hummer. After a heartbeat, Courtney followed.

"You weren't kidding when you said her dad didn't like you."

"I don't get that. He should like me; everybody should like me. You like me, right?" I asked her, trying to break the tension.

Crickets.

"Dick, you're a nice guy in your own way, but you have this… killer instinct… no, that's not it… deadly fog… no… Um…"

"I'm a living and breathing shit magnet?" I asked her.

She snapped her fingers and pointed at me, "That's it!"

"Great," I said, and fired up the Hummer and drove through the gate.

We were both aware that the old man was staring at the Hummer, looking into it as we drove past. I waited, and when he got the gate closed, he climbed on the quad and turned it around.

"Follow me," he said, and took off.

"You nervous?" Courtney asked me rhetorically.

I managed a nod and swallowed a lump in my throat. I started down the driveway slowly, and her hand covered my right hand that was on the shifter, and gave it a gentle squeeze.

"You're going to be ok," she said quietly.

I couldn't respond. I was even more nervous than the first time I'd asked a girl to a school dance. If I strained, I thought I might remember her name, but I was too focused on not crashing the Hummer. It was that hard, every muscle was so tense, and even turning the steering wheel was an agony of effort. Still, as we rounded the corner, I saw that the t-111 siding on the house had been painted a dark green, the same as the roof, and decided they'd probably done that in an effort to make the cabin not stand out from a distance.

I pulled up next to the old man and got out. The fields, the kitchen garden, even the small barn that held the one tractor and workshop was all the same. Everything was lush green, and for being so far out in the middle of nowhere, they had grown up used to going without power. Their homestead and farm had been built in a time when there was no power.

I saw a feminine figure walking out of the woods with a young boy and I smiled, standing there awkwardly, but feeling the tension ebb away. She was a way off, but she looked up as if at some-
232

thing the boy said, and I could see her squint. She all but threw what looked like a .22 into the surprised boy's hands, and took off at a mad dash. The boy shrugged and turned to walk back toward the way he'd come. I wanted to run out there, but I was rooted to the spot. The old man looked at me, and then Maggie, and his scowl cracked, and he gave me and Courtney a grin.

"He loves that little girl something fierce," the old man said, then turned toward the house where I heard a door bang open.

Mom and Mary stood there. Mary's jaw dropped open and she took off at a jog toward me. I looked to my left, Maggs. To my right, Mary. Everything I had fought for, everything I'd wanted.

Maggie got within ten feet of me, outpacing her mother and seemingly launched herself into the air like Superman. She tackled me to the ground and tried to squeeze the air out of me. I hugged back as hard as I could and tried to get up. She'd grown so big. She was no longer the little girl I'd remembered. It had been so long. Tears threatened to overtake me and I stood, holding onto her with her head buried in my neck. Mary stood before me and Courtney had tears running down her cheeks.

"You made it. I thought… a long time ago, I thought you'd be…"

"Uncle Mike, I'm so glad you made it back home!"

"Who's Uncle Mike?" Courtney asked.

Everyone looked at her and then to me, and I let go of Maggs as I fainted.

BOYD CRAVEN

* * *

"How long have you been off your meds?" Mary asked me as a cool washcloth wiped at my face.

I startled awake and tried to sit up. I'd fainted in the grass, in front of the Hummer.

"I… Um…" My throat was dry, and my memories were a swirling mess.

"Wait, he's Mike? Then, who's Dick?" Courtney asked, a heavy dose of anxiety dripping from her words.

"Dick was my husband. He served with Mike here. He was killed in action and Mike here tried to… I mean," Mary's words choked up.

I sat up and felt for the pocket that held the picture. I pulled the flap and held up the picture.

"Yes, that's the picture Dick was looking at when he died. You promised him that you'd bring it back to us," Mary said softly. "Can you get up?"

Somehow I could, and did.

"Somebody tell me what's going on?" Courtney said with a quiver in her voice that I didn't like. It was fear. Fear and uncertainty.

"Come inside, dear," Mom said. "This isn't the first time. Pops, make sure he don't fall again. He's got so much gear on this time, you'd think he'd fought a war."

"Um… he sort of did," Courtney said, but she was following.

The old man had me by the back of the pants and Mom had an arm around my shoulders. Normally, this wouldn't be possible because she was

234

only as tall as Maggs, but my legs didn't want to straighten and they felt watery.

"Well, that's par for the course. Come on with us and we'll explain."

"Is he going to be all right?" Maggie asked nobody in particular.

"He will be," Pops said. "He's a tough old bastard."

* * *

How long had I been off my meds? The pieces were starting to fall into place. I was Mike. Dick Pershing, I was not. But I'd been Dick for so long, at least in my mind, that it was difficult to make things out.

"I really need to know what's going on," Courtney said, helping Mary pull off my vest, and then all of the gear I had strapped to me, until I was down to a t-shirt and my pants.

"What do you know about PTSD?" Mary asked.

"I don't know, I'm not a psychologist."

"Well, I am. I'm not asking you to be snarky or rhetorical, but it would help if I knew what your understanding of it was."

"Oh… um… stress from having seen or done bad things?"

"That's close enough," she said. "Mike here has a bad case of it, plus he's also been diagnosed with Schizoaffective disorder."

I tried not to cry when I saw Courtney flinch.

"Mike lost not only both of his best friends, he killed one of them directly. When he was captured and tortured by the Taliban, it really did a number on him."

"Do you remember all of this?" Courtney asked me.

"Pieces. Incomplete pieces to a puzzle." I did not remember the torture, maybe in time, but that one was new to me.

"Why did you think you were Dick?"

I felt in my pocket and the picture wasn't there. I started getting frantic, and I was about to roll off the bed when Courtney handed it to me. She'd been holding onto it, keeping it safe.

I flattened the slightly bent picture out, looking at the bloody thumbprint. Dick's thumbprint.

"Part of that is my fault," Mary said, not meeting either of our eyes.

"Why is that?" I asked her.

"Because for a time, I thought I'd fallen in love with you."

Memories came crashing back. The days and weeks of recovery. My escape from the Taliban. Setting up an ambush because I had forty of them running after me. Using the same trap and ambush techniques I'd been taught by King, to whittle their numbers down in order to escape, only to have the fragments of an IED or grenade hit me, just as I got within sight of a US military base. Then, I'd woken up bloody, bandaged, and with no idea where I had been. I had memories of killing James, of failing Dick and letting him bleed out, while I'd exacted my revenge on the man who'd been part of the ambush at the bank, when we'd been under sniper fire.

236

THE DEVIL'S DUE

Somebody took my hand, and when I looked, it wasn't Mary. It was Courtney. She gave me a squeeze as if to encourage me. Not all of it was fake. Not all of it was false memories. I did love Mary, and for all intents and purposes, Maggie was my daughter. The wife and child of my best friend. We'd fallen in love, I thought, and then I'd let the darkness overtake me.

"Dick… er… Mike… I don't know what to call you." Courtney started sobbing.

"Do you have my box?" I asked Mary.

"Yes, I never threw it away. Even after they said that you had died."

"I keep hearing about me being dead, but it keeps not happening."

"Dick Pershing really is dead," Courtney told me, giving my hand another squeeze.

"Oh, man. This…"

"I'll be right back," Mary said, getting up, her eyes glistening.

I sat up and coughed. It hurt, down deep. The memories were coming back; so quick, so fast. Of making love to Mary in this very bed. Of fishing with Maggs, of endless doctor's appointments with Mary at my side… both before we were together and after. The thing that killed me though, was that deep down, somewhere in my dreams, I'd always known the truth. As ugly and horrible as the dreams about James had been, he'd told me plainly. He'd reminded me of who I really was. The horrible ugly truth had been there the whole time and I'd ignored it, in favor of my delusions.

237

BOYD CRAVEN

"You're still a good man," Courtney said. "Even if you're not who you think you were."

"Why aren't you running and screaming? I'm damaged goods. Crazy. Coo coo."

"Because I think you need a friend right now. Somebody who understands the darkness inside."

"I do," I told her, squeezing her hand back.

"Does Maggie know?"

"That me and her mom...?"

"Yeah."

"I think she suspected, but it was such a short period of time. It was during the heroin days for me."

"Daze?"

"No, days. The days I lost to drugs. I stayed away from them. I couldn't... didn't want them to see that. Didn't want anyone to see that. It's... there's a lot. I don't know what's real."

I felt her squeeze my hand again, and I looked up to see her eyes were tear-streaked, like everyone else.

"What now?"

"I don't know. I don't know if I'll even remember who I am next week."

That was when Mary walked back in. Her eyes were red, but she had finished her crying in the hallway, where her parents and Maggie waited. I opened the Nike shoebox, and inside were four rubber-banded stacks of photos. I pulled them out and set them on the bed. One by one, I started going through them. Mary would help remind me who the people were in the photos, the places I didn't

238

recognize, but other than that... This was my life.

I suddenly remembered where I'd seen them, at the hospital when I had been restrained. It had been a year before the EMP had hit. I had showed up at the farm, strung out and lost. Mary had had me committed until I'd been deemed safe enough to be released, knowing that if I went off my meds, quit therapy and went back to drugs, it was only a small stopgap. In a fit of clarity, I'd asked her to hold onto my personal belongings so if I ever showed up again in a confusion, I'd be able to find my way back home.

Maggie walked in, ignoring a death glare from her mom and plopped on the bed next to me, crowding Courtney out of the way. Courtney wanted to give her a dirty look, but a smile was tugging at the corners of her mouth. Stay with somebody long enough, day after day, you learn their body language. Still, the kid had some 'cajones' to bust in and ignore the ladies' ugly looks. Instead, she grabbed the pictures out of the stack and started shuffling them, till she held one up.

In it, Dick and I were standing side-by-side, wearing button up denim shirts, blue jeans, and sporting cowboy hats. He had an AR and I was holding a KSG, the one I still carried. In it, Maggie was barely big enough to look over the top of the shooting bench that was on the far side of the property, overlooking the looming hill.

"This is where you and my daddy taught me how to shoot," she said, turning to look me in the eyes and smiling. "Do you remember, Uncle Mike?"

I did, and I nodded.

"You remember the advice you gave me that day?"

"Don't point your guns at nothing you don't want to kill," I told her.

She nodded. "Unless, it was an annoying boy." She grinned.

"Wait, that was your dad who said that."

She shrugged. Maybe I wasn't the only one who mixed up events in my mind.

"I don't really want to shoot anybody, but when I saw the picture box coming out I wanted to show you, and to see how big I really was back then. I've been teaching the boys around here how to shoot. They want to join up with the local militias."

"Maggie!" Mary said, anger creeping into her voice.

With that, her mom and dad stepped inside the bedroom.

"Well, it's true. The President has been talking about the attacks on the radios. They're in Texas. As long as that boy who stinks doesn't try anything, he'll be safe... but I might have to shoot him with Momma's BB gun, if he doesn't stop."

"Does this stinky boy have a younger brother?" I asked her.

"You talking about Russell?" Her cheeks turned bright red.

"Here we go again," Courtney said, standing up and flinging her hands into the air.

Mary looked to Courtney, her daughter, and then to me.

THE DEVIL'S DUE

"What?" Mary asked after a minute.

"Is there some kinda local dance being set up around these parts?" I asked.

"Yeah, we're talking about having it a week from tonight, actually. Almost like an early Thanksgiving, but it's more about the harvest time," Mary's father said.

Maggs looked at me intently.

"Russell plans on stealing a kiss at the dance," I said, feeling wicked for enjoying the sight of Mary's eyes flaring wide in anger.

Her father started chuckling, but was biffed in the stomach by her mom. "I'll shoot him with the BB gun, myself!" she said.

I cracked up. In a moment, everyone but Maggie was cracking up.

"You going to be around long enough to shoot the kid for me, Mike?" Mom asked.

"If you'll have me for a time."

"Well shit, you're almost family. We'll just have to fix up a bedroom for you and your lady friend. You both can bunk in the one near the furnace.

Courtney shot me a puzzled look.

"It's in the basement. Warmest spot in the house in the winter," I told her.

"The winter is coming, Jon Snow," Maggie intoned.

I looked at everyone, confused. They laughed.

* * *

I'd spent so much time thinking I was someone

241

else, spent so long pining after a girl I couldn't have, that it felt weird waking up next to Courtney. There was no more awkwardness between us. Part of me still ached for Jamie, the only woman other than Mary that I had felt love for, but with time, talking with Mary and going through my memory box, life came back to me slowly. I felt more complete than I could remember. When I woke up from a nightmare, Courtney would be there to calm me, ground me. Together, we were both mourning in our own ways, and learning how to move on.

I thought at first it might be weird for Mary, but I found out that she'd remarried and then been widowed again in the last few years. She was still too raw to think about me any way, other than a friend, and once things started clicking into place, I realized I felt the same. Losing the woman I'd thought I'd loved to false memories, didn't hurt as bad as it should. I won't lie. I missed Jamie, and on more than one occasion as I rested and healed my mind, I found myself getting the radio out and staring at it. Wanting to call her. The biggest thing I'd learned from living in the sewers of Chicago with my motley crew of family, then journeying across the country, was that no matter how bad things seemed, it can and does get better - if you try.

This may not have been how I expected to view this day, but I had my surrogate daughter, two ladies who thought fondly of me, some almost-parents who had put up with me, and a lot of memories to sift through. Out of the darkness, I'd found my light. I'd found my faith and I'd found my direction

242

THE DEVIL'S DUE

in life again. Soon, we'd be heading to Texas. There would be no rest, until the New Caliphate was put down.

"Dick, are you still up?" Courtney asked me from the darkness, her hand rubbing my shoulder the way she would when I'd awaken from a nightmare.

"Yeah, but I'm going to sleep now," I said, and lay down next to her.

Two friends, finding the light together.

–THE END–

AUTHOR'S NOTE

I want to thank everyone for following my characters through this trilogy. I want to say up front that I've never served myself, and any and all screw ups are mine and mine alone.

I'm sure somebody out there can think of someone like Dick. Some may have it better, some may have it worse, but we've all seen what mental health issues, substance abuse and PTSD can do to a person and family.

Keep our veterans in your thoughts and prayers, if you are a prayer warrior. Without them and many like them since the birth of our country, freedom wouldn't be what it is today in the USA.

Now, I did finish this trilogy, and although I won't be writing more in Dick's world directly, follow up in reading The World Burn's Series. Book 9 is currently being written, and it bridges the gaps between books 1 and two. The World Burns 10 should tie things in all nicely, and Dick and Courtney may be back in cameo, doing what they do best:

Blowing up bad guys and trying to heal. A friendship forged through the fires of horror, pain, loss and grief, yet never ending friends forever.

Thanks for reading!!

Boyd

ABOUT THE AUTHOR

Boyd Craven III has penned over 20 books over the last two years, only recently deciding to take the plunge into publishing. His "The World Burns" Series has hit the top 10 in the Dystopian Genre in the USA, the UK, Canada and Australia. Boyd has made his home in Michigan with his wonderful wife and about a million kids, but travels to Texas to visit family as frequently as possible.

He hunts and goes fishing when he's not dreaming up post-apocalyptic nightmares to put his characters through. Fear not though, Boyd is a huge believer that in the darkest hour, there is always a glimmer of hope to hold onto.

In addition to being a modern day urban farmer, Boyd belongs to a co-op selling at the local farmers market, and lately has been experimenting with living off the grid - an excellent way to research for his series, as well as torture his teenage sons.

Prepare yourself by reading his books - they're a thrill ride, on or off the grid.

http://www.amazon.com/Boyd-Craven-III/e/B00BANIQLG/